COWBOY LOST

KINGS OF MONTANA, BOOK 2

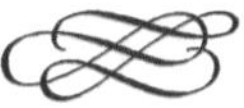

VANESSA GRAY BARTAL

DRY CREEK PRESS

One look and he knew he didn't like her. She stood frozen scanning the horizon with her high heels, faultlessly coiffed tresses, and cool reserve. Piercing crystal blue eyes gave her a frosty appearance, and the style of her flaxen hair did nothing to change that impression. Her long mane was secured tightly at the base of her neck, pulling her features taut; her azure eyes were wide and unsmiling. Not a hair was out of place, not a wrinkle dared appear on her clothing. She was perfect—perfectly cold. He remained in the shadows a minute observing her haughty expression through narrowed eyes before stepping forward to introduce himself.

"Ivy?" He said it like a question, although he knew it was her. Not only had he seen her picture, but she was the only person his age at the airport.

She turned toward him, her frigid expression unwavering. "Josh?" Her tone was questioning, too.

He shook his head. "Josh couldn't make it. I'm Coy."

If anything, the look on her face became even more distant. "Coy," she repeated his name the same way she might have said *cockroach.* "You're the twin."

"I'm the twin," he agreed, silently cursing his twin brother, Cam. If not for him, he wouldn't be in this uncomfortable situation. If not for him, this interfering snob wouldn't be intruding on their ranch for the next two weeks. If not for Cam, their lives would remain peaceful and unaltered, like always. But for once in his life, the ever-sensible Cameron had lost his head over a girl. *This* girl, nonetheless. Although, he hadn't lost it far enough to put aside business long enough to retrieve her from the airport. Oh, no, for that he had to condemn Coy to a three hour car ride with the ice queen of Kentucky.

"We should get your bags," he said.

She nodded, clutching her two carry-on bags tighter as if she were afraid he might take them from her. She needn't have worried. The bags were small and light, and he saw no need to relieve her of them. He would carry the larger bags once they retrieved them from the luggage carousel.

Generally he was never at a loss for small talk, but there was a first time for everything. He wracked his brain for something to say to her. *Are you as boring as Cam makes you sound? If you smile, does your face crack from the shock? Were you born in a dress and high heels, or does it only seem that way? Are you going to throw a fit the first time you get your shoes dirty on the ranch and realize it's not mud you stepped in?*

That last question made him smile as he imagined her reaction to the ranch. Their spread was vast and wild, certainly no place for the likes of Her Royal Highness. Maybe Cam would retain his patience for her once he saw how ill-suited she was to ranch life, but Coy wouldn't put up with any whining. His good cheer increased once he realized he wouldn't have to. This was Cam's girl, not his. After this day was over, he could go about his business and pretend she didn't exist. He could do anything for three hours—even spend the time with someone he despised at first sight. With that happy thought in mind, he pursed his lips and started to whistle.

* * *

Ivy wasn't sure what to think of her chauffer. Perhaps she shouldn't think of him in those terms, but at the moment she was disinclined to think of him as anything else. He might be Cameron King's fraternal twin brother, but he had made it clear he wanted nothing to do with her. Much to her chagrin, Cam had relayed Coy's less than thrilled reaction to the news of their relationship. And now Ivy was seeing it up close and in person. To say he loathed her would be putting it mildly. Added to the fact that she was jetlagged by flying west, along with the confusing two-hour time difference, she was not in a great mood. She was tired. She was hungry. She had a headache, and her feet were killing her. She couldn't wait to take her shoes off and eat, in that order.

Ivy's doubts and misgivings over this vacation returned en force. Her first inclination was to bite her lip, but that might reveal some of what she was feeling to Coy, and she was too unsure of his hostility to show any weakness in front of him. So she remained stoic, forcing her face into the signature calm expression years of dealing with her family had taught her.

If only Cam had been the one to retrieve her from the airport. In theory, she understood he was the boss of his massive ranch. She understood the fact that he needed to be present to meet a large shipment of new cattle arriving at the ranch. She understood he wanted to be the one to transition them to their new surroundings and acclimate them to the ranch. In theory, she didn't begrudge him the call of duty.

But there was a small part of her that was hurt by his absence. They had been talking over the internet for the past twelve months. Each transmission had grown until they had a true, fledgling relationship. She hadn't invited herself to the ranch; she had come when he beckoned her. Was it really too much to ask that he take one day off from work to meet her at the airport? If he had been here to meet her, he probably would have picked her up in a massive bear hug. Maybe he would have kissed her. Even if he had simply shaken her hand it would have been preferable to Coy's cold greeting. She was amazed at the self control that kept him from sneering when he said her name.

The unfairness of the situation hit her anew, making her want to stomp her feet and pound her fists. She hadn't done anything to him, why did he dislike her so? Obviously he was suspicious of her and wary for his brother's sake, but she hadn't sought Cam. He had found her online and pursued her. Every move in their tentative relationship had been his. How was Ivy the bad guy in this scenario?

If she were being honest with herself, she probably wouldn't much care for Coy even if he had been warm and friendly to her. He reminded her too much of her older brothers, all five of them. Growing up, they had made her life a living nightmare. Some girls dreamed of having five older brothers; Ivy dreamed of being an only child. Only children didn't have to be teased mercilessly over every blessed thing. Only children didn't have their first bra taken to school and run up the flagpole. Only children didn't have their diaries stolen and read out loud over supper. One of the things that had attracted her to Cameron in the first place was his quiet, serious nature. He wasn't one to tease, and she was tempted to marry him for that fact alone. From Cam's first description of his twin, though, she had known Coy was a teaser. And she hadn't liked him.

Apparently whatever Cam had told his brother about her had made the feeling mutual. She wondered suddenly what Cam had told Coy to make him dislike her so much, but she wasn't going to ask and find out. The less said between them, the better. All she had to do was survive the three hour ride to the ranch and then she would be safely ensconced in Cam's arms, figuratively speaking. From what she knew of him, he wasn't the touchy-feely type, but that was okay. Their relationship was new. They would take things slowly. As long as they wove in a few gentle kisses before she left, she would be happy.

Beside her, Coy's glacial glare suddenly turned into a warm smile. Startled, she looked around to see what might have caused the transformation. Had he seen a pretty girl? There was no one besides them, though. Whatever caused his mood shift must have been internal, but she wasn't complaining. At least he looked approachable when he smiled, not that she had any plans to talk to him. When he started to whistle, she turned her head to the side and tried not to roll her eyes.

They walked in silence until they reached the luggage carousel. Ivy pointed out her two large suitcases. He muttered incoherently under his breath, probably something about the size of her bags. Instead of explaining to him she was spending two whole weeks here and needed everything she had brought, she remained silent. And then he said something that caused her blood to freeze in fury.

"If I touch these, are they going to make me itch, Poison Ivy?"

CHAPTER 2

From birth, Ivy had learned not to react to teasing. She knew from her brothers a reaction was what they wanted, especially an angry reaction. But if there was one thing guaranteed to get under her skin, it was being called Poison Ivy—a nickname she had been stuck with all her life. By the wicked gleam in Coy's eye, she knew he was waiting for her to react, so she didn't.

"They're a little heavy. Don't put your back out," she said, very sweetly if she did say so herself. Then she turned away to hide her smirk of satisfaction when he grunted as he lifted her suitcases to the ground. Her head rose imperiously as she walked in front of him, feeling very good about her self-control.

"Uh, do you know where you're going?" Coy called from behind her.

She stopped short and looked around, befuddled. The airport wasn't as large as the one she had left in Lexington, but it was still large enough she had no idea where she was headed. Pressing her lips together, she stood back and waited for him to pass her.

"That's what I thought," he muttered, loudly enough for her to hear. She stuck her tongue out at the back of his head.

The walk to the truck was silent and short. Both of them were as anxious as possible to get the day over with so they could get away from each other. That made what she was about to say next all the more intolerable.

"Would you mind if we grab something to eat before we go?"

Now it was his turn to press his lips together, probably to stop his lip from curling. "Layla will have supper waiting for us when we arrive home."

Layla, she knew, was their housekeeper. She was also his brother Cade's girlfriend. Ivy was somewhat leery about meeting the other girl. Having spent most of her life with boys, she wasn't sure how she would be received. And she certainly didn't want to do anything to make a bad impression. On the other hand, she was starving.

"I'll be hungry again in three hours," she promised. "There was no food on the plane. I haven't eaten since five this morning." She hated adding that last part, hated copping to any weakness, even hunger. But the plain truth was she was as hungry as she had ever been. Her blood sugar was low, adding to her headache and ill temper.

Coy ran a weary hand over his face. "To tell you the truth, I could go for something, too. Is it all right if we hit a drive through? I'm trying to stay ahead of the weather."

She waited until she had hefted herself into the tall truck to respond. "The weather?"

He nodded. "It's what happens when atmospheric changes occur."

Her teeth ground together in an effort to keep from snapping at him. "I'm aware of the definition of the word. Is there bad weather moving in? It's only October."

"Welcome to Montana. There are basically two seasons: spring and winter." He darted a glance in her direction. "Don't look so worried, city slicker. We're well prepared for bad weather here. And it's only supposed to be a few inches—nothing unmanageable. I'm simply being cautious so I can deliver you to my brother unharmed."

And then immediately wash your hands of me, she added mentally. She wanted to tell him she wasn't a city slicker, but she held her tongue. Again—a feat which was becoming more difficult by the minute. *Three hours,* she reminded herself. *Three hours and then I can ignore him for the next two weeks.*

He pulled into a fast food burger joint. From what she could tell, there were only a handful of fast food places in the entire town, a far cry from the cities she was used to in Kentucky. Some of his reasoning for calling her a city slicker was starting to become apparent. Although she thought of herself as a country girl for her rural digs, there was rural, and then there was *rural.* The house where she grew up was surrounded by a few other houses and a whole lot of fields. She had a feeling the King ranch house would be the only domicile in sight for miles. Coy placed his order, startling her out of her reverie.

"I'll have two cheeseburgers, a large soda, large fries, and a chocolate milkshake." He finished speaking into the box and looked questioningly at her.

"I'll have the same," she said.

He sputtered a laugh. "Are you serious?"

"I told you I'm hungry," she said.

Still laughing, he turned back to the box and doubled his order. She reached for her purse, but he stilled her with his hand.

"What are you doing?"

"Paying," she said.

He frowned at her, took out his wallet, and paid the girl at the first window. "Put that away," he commanded, pointing at her purse.

With a sigh, she complied. The guys she knew in Kentucky had no trouble with her paying her way. She was beginning to think she had landed in another century, and not another state. Her suspicion grew when Coy turned his attention on the girl behind the cash register.

"How you doing today, sweetness?"

The girl blushed and giggled before dropping his change on the ground. She bent to retrieve it and bonked her head on the corner of the counter, knocking her netted hat askew. By the time she handed him his change, her face was magenta with mortification. Unruffled by the exchange, Coy calmly drove to the next window to retrieve their food. Once again it was a girl, and once again he made her a nervous wreck by flirting outrageously with her. Ivy's conviction she had chosen the correct brother was becoming stronger by the minute. If there was one thing she disliked as much as a teaser, it was a flirt. Coy was both in one smug little package.

He accelerated out of the drive-thru while he handed her their food. "Could you sort that for us?" When she didn't respond, he glanced at her before pulling out onto the road. "What?"

"Nothing," she said. It was none of her business he was the biggest flirt west of the Mississippi. He was her sort-of boyfriend's twin brother, and nothing more. She felt slightly affronted for females everywhere, but beyond that she didn't care what he did. Or with whom.

"If you have something on your mind you'd better say it," he said.

So he didn't like it when people didn't spill their every thought and emotion. Interesting. She smiled. "Whatever do you mean? I've never been happier." She sifted through the bag and handed him a sandwich.

He regarded her with a subdued expression, but she could see the anger and dislike simmering below the surface. "Butter wouldn't melt in your mouth," he said.

Meaning she was cold, she guessed. She almost laughed at that. If her brothers could hear anyone describe her as cool and reserved they would no doubt die from laughing so hard. Funnier still, Coy thought he was insulting her, but he was actually paying her a compliment. She had worked long and hard to be able to rein in her unwieldy emotions. Apparently her hard work was paying off.

"Thank you for the sandwiches," she said easily. "They're delicious." And then before she could tempt herself into baiting him further, she dug into her food and didn't say another word until she was finished.

COY COULDN'T BELIEVE she ate the whole thing. At first he thought maybe she was ordering so much to be contrary. At any moment he expected her to give up and leave the rest of her food for later. Then maybe he wondered if she was continuing out of pride, as a sort of competition with him. Finally he realized she simply had a healthy appetite. Oddly, that was a point in her favor. He had expected her to either be a vegetarian or one of those girls who only orders salad at dinner. Now he was left wondering where she put all of it. She was tall for a girl, probably 5'7", but she looked slim. Not skinny, but definitely not overweight.

And he had to admit her accent was kind of cute. He had never personally known anyone from the southeast before, so he had only ever heard the accent on television. He almost wanted to get her talking to listen to her softly lilting voice. Almost. For now he was enjoying the silence and hoping it would last. Since neither of them seemed compelled to break it, he turned on the radio.

She surprised him again when she began to quietly sing along. He had no idea why that should surprise him, except she seemed too pristine to do something as lowly as hum along with the radio. But when he was starting to waiver in his opinion of her, she went ahead and did something to reaffirm his dislike.

"You should wear your seatbelt," she said.

"I don't like to wear my seatbelt," he said. "It chafes my chest."

She blinked at him a few times, trying to determine if he was serious. Apparently he was. "It's the law."

"This is Montana. You're lucky if you see a cruiser in the entire state. I'm not worried about getting pulled over."

"Because there isn't an officer around to ticket you doesn't mean you don't have to follow the law," she said.

"Look, maybe you can boss Cam around, but you can't boss me."

"I don't boss Cam around, and I'm not bossing you either. I'm merely pointing out wearing your seatbelt is a good idea. An excellent idea, really."

When he made no move to reach for his seatbelt, she continued speaking.

"My cousin died in a car accident, okay? I get a little freaked out when I see someone not wearing his seatbelt. He would have lived if he had been wearing his."

After a few seconds of silence, he quietly reached over and fastened his safety belt.

"Thank you," she said softly. With that taken care of, she turned her attention to look out the window. No one had exaggerated the beauty of Montana. Every mile was like a picture on a postcard. There were a few houses, but no neighborhoods like she was used to. The towns were tiny with a gas station and post office taking up most of the space. Snow began softly falling and there was a pelting sound on the window. She wondered if there was ice mixing with the snow. Dusk was beginning to settle and Ivy was growing sleepy.

"We're only about a half hour from home now," Coy said. His voice sounded tense. He was leaning forward, gripping the steering wheel more tightly than he had before.

"Are the roads bad?"

"They're not great, but we'll make it. I've driven in worse. Nap if you want to."

A nap sounded heavenly right now. Her blinks grew heavier and heavier, and then her eyes popped open with a start.

What had Coy said? Goose? Loose? Then her eyes focused on the road and she suddenly understood his urgent tone. There in the middle of the road not four feet in front of them was the largest moose she had ever seen, which wasn't saying much because she had never seen a moose before. But she knew enough to realize if they hit the giant animal, they were done for.

Coy stomped the brake, sending the car into a fishtailed skid.

"Hold on," Coy said. Then they plunged over the steep ravine at the side of the road and began to descend.

CHAPTER 3

*T*imes like these, Ivy was glad she had never been a screamer. Long ago her brothers had killed any part of her that might be tempted to squeal like a little girl. Now she sat silently as they plummeted down the ravine at a death defying pace. There were unavoidable obstacles in the way, but they were small saplings. The large truck barreled over them as if they were paper. But at the bottom of the valley were larger, more deadly trees. If Coy was somehow unable to stop their progress before then, they were in real trouble.

As she was worrying about plummeting head first into a thirty-foot pine, a new worry began to take place. Because the ravine was so deep and the truck was heavier in the front than in the back, their tale end began leaving the ground with every bump. Now she began to fear the back end would lift so high they would flip end over end. Part of her wanted to squeeze her eyes tightly shut until it was over, but that felt like she was leaving Coy alone. She couldn't do that when he was fighting so hard to keep them alive.

And he *was* fighting hard. He had a death grip on the steering wheel and his foot pumped the brake as he simultaneously tried to slow their descent and keep them from hitting anything too big.

Trying to slow the car was futile on the loose, rocky terrain, but he was making a valiant effort. And so far he had steered them around a couple of large boulders that definitely would have sent them airborne.

At last they were at the bottom of the ravine and approaching the thick copse of trees. There was no gap big enough to drive through, and the truck was still going too fast. She glanced at Coy, saw him blinking furiously as he tried to calculate the risks and outcomes. Would they live if they hit a tree head on?

"Hold on," he yelled again, then he swung the wheel wildly to the right. Too late she saw what he intended to do. He was going to take the impact on his side, sparing her a hit.

"No," she yelled, but it was too late. The truck hit the tree with a sickening crunch. She lurched toward him. The seatbelt jerked her back. Her airbag deployed, and for a moment everything went black.

Thick smoke filled the truck and she coughed as she came to in a panic. Was the truck on fire? Frantically she waved her hand in front of her face to try and clear the air enough to see. With a sigh of relief she realized the smoke was simply powder from the airbags. She coughed again as the powder started to settle, then her relief was replaced by panic once again.

"Coy," she yelled. She waved her hand again, trying to clear the air between them. There was a part of her that didn't want to look, sure she would see his mangled body wrapped around a tree. But when she forced her eyes to focus, she saw the tree had hit right behind his door. The truck was partially wrapped around the large tree. Coy was unconscious with his bloody head resting against the cracked window.

"Coy," she repeated, more softly this time. She reached for him, but her seatbelt jerked her back once again. Swallowing a lump of panic, she released her seatbelt and crept toward him, her hand outstretched toward his neck. He was still warm and his pulse was strong, both good signs. She sat up on her knees and leaned as far over him as she could in order to inspect his head, the airbag pressed firmly against her back.

There was a massive amount of blood, but everyone knew head wounds tended to bleed a lot, so she wasn't put off by that. What frightened her was the fact that his head was what cracked the window. It took a lot of force to break a car window. With shaking fingers, she tentatively probed his head where it lay against the window, gently checking the area for cuts or lumps. She practically cried in relief when she felt a large goose egg at the exact spot where his head rested on the window. With head wounds, out was always better than in. The lump would no doubt be painful, but it was an indication things inside his skull were probably okay.

She let him go and retrieved a stack of napkins from their fast food bag. She pressed the napkins to the wound with gentle pressure, trying to stop the bleeding but not cause him further pain. Now she faced a dilemma. Should she try to wake him, or let him remain unconscious to avoid the pain? What if he had a concussion? Weren't people with concussions supposed to stay awake?

Before she could make up her mind, he groaned and began to stir. Not wanting to remove her hand and re-ignite the bleeding, she pressed her free hand to the uninjured side of his face.

"Coy, it's okay. Try to stay still. You're bleeding."

His eyes became slits as he tried to focus on her. He groaned again and licked his lips. "Who are you?" he whispered.

Oh, no. Did he have amnesia? "I'm Ivy," she said gently.

"That's right," he said. "Poison Ivy. What happened?"

Now was not the time to deal with the dreaded nickname, she reminded herself. Forcing patience into her tone, she tried to answer without any emotion. "There was a moose in the road. You went over a ravine to avoid hitting it."

He frowned. "Had to. Moose was too big. Would have died for sure."

Why was he explaining himself to her? "I know," she assured him. "You hit your head on the door when we crashed and it's bleeding. Are you injured anywhere else?"

"Dunno," he said. He blinked a couple of times to try and clear his head and slowly began moving his extremities, starting with his toes and working his way up. When he started to move his arms, there was an awkward pause when he realized she was leaning over him, impeding his movements and practically plastered to his chest.

"I can't let go of your head yet," she explained.

"'S okay," he said. He closed his eyes and rested his head on the seat behind him. "Think I'm fine. A little dazed."

"And bruised," she added.

"And bruised," he agreed. His eyes flew open and he sat up, wincing. "Are you okay?" He scanned her up and down, though he couldn't see much in the fading sunlight.

"I'm fine," she said. "I'm sure I'll have some sore muscles tomorrow, but otherwise I'm uninjured." She paused. "Thanks to you."

He closed his eyes and leaned back again, taking secret pleasure in her gratitude. Unfortunately, it was short-lived.

"What were you thinking?" she asked. "You could have been killed."

He frowned at her angry tone. "It was either me or you," he snapped.

"You could have hit it head on and given us both an equal shot," she said.

"An equal shot at death," he growled. "I can't believe you're arguing with me over this."

She drew in a breath and let it out slowly. "You're right. I'm sorry. Sometimes my temper gets the best of me."

He opened one eye and cocked it at her. "Really?" he drawled.

Drat. The secret was out now. No more fooling him into thinking she was cool as a cucumber. Without a doubt she knew as soon as he was better he would do everything in his power to get under her skin. She sighed in resignation; she supposed since he saved her life the least she could do was let him irritate her to death.

"It's mutual," he said after a pause.

"What?" She had no idea what he was talking about.

He plucked at the seatbelt. "If you hadn't made me wear this, I would be a goner for sure."

She shivered, not liking to think of what might have been. Silence returned, and it felt foreboding. She stared at the hill they had descended. From the bottom it looked like a mountain. She was amazed they survived. Outside the sun was almost finished setting and the snow was still falling. The truck had shut itself off when they slammed into the tree, and cold was already seeping in.

"What do we do now?" she asked, more to herself than to Coy.

"Nothing," he said. "We wait out the night right here. In the morning, I'll assess the situation and see what can be done. But there is no way to get up that hill in the dark with all this ice. We might die trying."

"And you're in no shape to go trekking up a cliff," she pointed out.

"I'm fine," he said, ignoring the fact that his face was a mask of pain.

Knowing it would do no good to point out he was far from fine, she turned her attention to practical matters. "I need to step outside for a minute."

"Don't go far from the truck," he warned.

"Don't peek," she said.

His only response was to chuckle. She slipped from the vehicle, literally. The ice on the ground had formed a thick layer. Her pretty shoes were no match for the weather. Holding on to the truck was the only thing that kept her upright. She squatted a few feet from the back right tire, thinking as she did so she had once vowed she would never again use the bathroom outside. When she was little, it was par for the course. Her brothers had no patience for differences in anatomy and never allowed her to return to the house to use the facilities, insisting instead she go wherever she happened to be—usually in the middle of a cornfield. As she grew and began to understand girls didn't drop their pants and go whenever the mood struck, she promised herself she would always find a toilet, no matter how far she had to go or how long she had to hold it.

But now she had no choice. They were stuck here for at least the next twelve hours until the sun came up. There was only so much holding a person could do. Despite her vow, she would never make it that long, especially not after all the soda she drank. Precariously, she picked her way back to the truck cab. As soon as she was inside, she turned to the seat beside her and began rifling through her carry-on backpack until she located her wet wipes.

After she cleaned her hands, she turned her attention to Coy and began gently sopping up the blood from the side of his face. To her immense relief, she noted the cut had stopped bleeding.

"How do you feel?" she asked. "Are you dizzy? Sick to your stomach? Any double vision?"

"I'm fine," he said without opening his eyes.

"Yes, you're very macho and I'm incredibly impressed by your bravery. Now how are you really?"

"My head hurts. Beyond that it's hard to think around the annoying buzz of voices in here."

He saved your life and he's injured. Don't punch him, she told herself. Instead, she rifled through her bag and shook out a couple of pain relievers. Picking up his soda, she held it out to him along with the pills. "Take these."

"Thanks," he said. He threw back the pills, took a sip of soda, and closed his eyes again.

"Can I get you anything else?" she offered.

"Silence," he whispered, grimacing in pain once again.

She closed her mouth and faced forward, then jumped in surprise when he rested his fingers in her forearm.

"Sorry. I know I'm being a bear. Head really hurts."

"'S okay," she said, imitating his earlier slurred speech. He smiled and relaxed slightly. "I'm going to change clothes," she whispered. "No peeking."

"No peeking," he agreed, also in a whisper.

"Promise?" she asked.

"Promise," he agreed, and then he fell asleep.

CHAPTER 4

$\mathcal{I}$vy took her time changing clothes while Coy slept. She had to; her fingers were already beginning to numb from the cold. How could it be so cold here in early October? It was uncanny.

She warmed slightly after she traded her lightweight sweater set for a hoodie and her tailored pants for some sturdy jeans. Taking off the painful yet pretty high heels was blessed relief. She wanted to sing when she put on her thick wool socks and comfortable hiking boots. Because she had nothing else to do, she also used a wet wipe to remove her makeup and wash her face. Then she brushed her teeth using a tiny amount of some leftover bottled water from her bag. Belatedly it occurred to her they might need every ounce of water they could get in the coming hours. Thankfully, they had both ordered large sodas with their meals. Half of hers was left, and Coy was down to a quarter of a cup. Thinking of their lack of liquid made her thirsty, but she told herself it was psychological and denied herself a sip.

To relieve her restless boredom, she released her hair from its confines and brushed it a few times before putting her toiletries away. The cold was becoming pervasive now. She was worried about Coy. It seemed unnatural he should fall asleep so quickly and easily so soon after returning to consciousness. She was worried he might be injured worse than she realized or in shock.

Once again she turned to the back seat and began rifling through her clothes, looking for a way to cover him. She dug out her coat, thinking it was pitifully lightweight for this dreadful weather. With a shiver of her own, she laid it over Coy. He stirred and looked at her in the dim moonlight.

"Who are you?" he asked.

Not again, she thought. Did he suffer from memory loss every time he woke?

Sensing her confusion, he continued. "When I fell asleep you looked like a different person." A short while ago she had looked like a sorority girl. Now she looked like someone he might go out and toss a ball with. She wore a hoodie he assumed to be blue because it had the University of Kentucky logo on it. She also wore jeans and—surprise, surprise—hiking boots on her feet. Even more stunning was the fact that they looked completely broken in and not as if she had bought them for this trip. Somehow, she looked younger, fresher. He wondered if maybe she had removed her makeup. He knew for sure she had taken down her hair. He liked her like this. She was much more approachable this way.

He shifted uncomfortably and realized he was covered by a thin coat. "Is this your coat?"

"No, it's hers." She pointed to the empty back seat.

He laughed and winced. "Smart mouth. What sort of ridiculous getup is this? It's not enough to keep you warm."

"In Kentucky it's still seventy degrees. How was I to know I was entering Antarctica?"

"Didn't Cam tell you to be prepared for cold weather?"

"Yes, he did. But I thought he meant normal fall cold weather. Not dead of winter where the sun doesn't shine cold weather."

"I'm not sure you understand what the phrase 'where the sun doesn't shine' means."

"I think I do," she replied, making him laugh and wince again. He threw off her coat and sat up. He leaned over to reach below the seat, but the world pitched and he paused.

She rested her palm on his back. "What are you doing?"

"Getting something under the seat."

"Sit back, stupid, before you pass out." She manhandled him into an upright position and pressed his shoulders back against the seat. He took a couple of deep breaths, trying to regain his equilibrium.

"Did you call me stupid?" he asked when he could talk.

"Good, your hearing is working well," she replied. "Wish I could say the same for the rest of your brain. You have a head injury. What are you thinking bending over like that?"

"I was thinking I need to get something from beneath the seat," he replied testily. His pride stung more from his incapacitation than from her stifling condescension. If he were being honest, he would admit he found her concern a little gratifying.

She gave a prolonged sigh. "In the future, please tell me when you want something and I will get it for you. Now what am I looking for under here?" She leaned down and began to sift her hand under the seat.

"It's a metal emergency kit," he said.

"Emergency kit," she said. The sound was muffled by the seat. "That's handy."

"This is Montana. We come prepared, which is more than I can say for the people of Kentucky."

She sat up and scowled at him. "The people of Kentucky are prepared for Kentucky-type emergencies."

"What are Kentucky-type emergencies?" he asked.

She leaned over again. "Still explosions. Moonshine shortages. Running out of cousins to marry. That sort of thing."

He laughed so hard he crossed his arms over his stomach and groaned. "Oh, stop making me laugh. It hurts."

She sat up again. "What hurts?"

"Everything. Did you find the box?"

"Yes, it's invisible now. Here you go." She pretended to set something on his lap.

He laughed and groaned again. "What are you waiting for?" He made a shooing motion with his hand toward the floor of the truck.

"For the stupid questions to stop," she muttered as she bent over once again.

He smiled at the top of her head, trying to remember when he had laughed so much or so hard in such a short period of time. And to think it was the snobby ice princess who made it happen. Maybe while he was out she switched places with someone else. Maybe she was a twin, too. How else to explain the differences in her?

At last she located the emergency kit and pulled it out. She set it on the seat between them and opened it.

"I can't see a thing," she complained.

"I can tell you what's in it," he said. Then, without being asked, he began to rattle off the contents of the kit. "Two bottles of water, some nuts that are probably stale by now, a first aid kit, extra ammunition, matches, and two emergency blankets."

"Ammunition," she repeated.

"Don't tell me you don't have guns in Kentucky," he said.

"Of course we do," she said. "I was simply trying to figure out if the bullets were for us in case the fighting gets too bad."

He sputtered a laugh that ended on a groan. "At this rate you won't need bullets to do me in. You're going to amuse me to death."

"That's the plan," she said. She began feeling around inside the kit, trying to locate the blankets.

Guessing her intent, he decided to offer her a tip. "You won't feel any material. These are those foil-type blankets. They're folded up in a tiny, plastic package."

"Gotcha," she said. He wasn't sure if she was talking to him or the blankets, but a few seconds later she pulled out two small plastic pouches and began opening them. When she couldn't open them with her fingers, she used her teeth to tear them open. Pulling out the first blanket, she covered him, taking care to tuck the blanket all around him. He could have done it himself, but he was sort of amused by watching her fuss over him. But when she pulled out the second blanket and covered him with that, too, he put his foot down.

"Oh no you don't. That one is for you," he said.

"But you're injured," she protested.

"I'm fine," he insisted.

"Yes, that bloody goose egg sings good health," she said sarcastically. "I'll be fine. I have my coat." She picked up the flimsy coat from where it had fallen on the floor.

"That's not a coat, it's a few strings banded together. Take a blanket. No discussion."

She grabbed one of the blankets and tucked it around herself. "I would say the head wound is making you grouchy, but I happen to know you were like this before."

That made him smile, but he tried to hide it. "Actually, you might be surprised to learn I'm usually thought of as a pleasant, happy-go-lucky person. Must be something making me grumpy. Or rather someone."

"I'm choosing to ignore your rude behavior because you're weak and infirm." She guessed correctly any reminder of his temporary limitation would be a swat at his pride.

"I'm fine," he repeated, crossing his arms over his chest. "I have this lingering headache that has more to do with the chatterbox in the truck than the cut and bump."

"I'm not a chatterbox," she said sulkily, crossing her arms over her chest. She was intensely uncomfortable and wished for bucket seats so she could recline. Instead, the seat was more like a couch so they were both stuck sitting up all night.

"Sleep tight, Poison Ivy," Coy whispered. He rested his head against his door and closed his eyes.

She studied him in silence, but she couldn't see much because of the gathering darkness. Finally when she could hold her temper no longer, she opened her mouth and whispered, "Coy, when you get better, I swear I'm going to punch your lights out."

At first she wasn't sure he had heard her, then she realized his shoulders were shaking with silent laughter. Feeling a little better, she smiled, closed her eyes, and tried to go to sleep.

CHAPTER 5

There was an odd clicking sound. Ivy woke with a start when she realized it was her teeth chattering together. She had slid down so her cheek was pressed to the window, and now that side of her face was numb with cold.

"What's the matter?" Coy whispered. His voice sounded stronger and more coherent, much to her relief.

"N-nothing," she stuttered. Stupid frozen lips, why wouldn't they work properly? She wasn't sure she had ever been this cold in her life. "Wh-what time is it-t?"

Coy held up his watch and tried to read it in the dim moonlight. "A little after midnight."

She nodded, sat up, and flexed her sore muscles. It took her a moment to remember why she was sore, and then the accident came flooding back. The seatbelt had jerked her entire body when they hit the tree. No doubt she was going to have some lingering soreness for a couple of days, but it was nothing she couldn't handle. "How's your head?" she asked Coy. "Truthfully," she added so he wouldn't be tempted to give her the same macho "I'm fine" he had been using all night.

"It hurts, but not unbearably. I feel better than before." He sighed.

"I hate to say it, but I have to use the facilities. Prepare yourself for a cold blast."

She wasn't sure she could get any colder, but she was wrong. As soon as he opened the door, an arctic blast of cold, combined with swirling snow, entered the truck. She wrapped her arms around herself and rubbed her hands up and down them to try and chafe some warmth back into herself. Coy returned a few minutes later and she squeezed her eyes shut when he opened the door again.

He settled himself in the truck and, even in the darkness, she could see him shivering, too.

"You're not going to like what I'm about to say," he said.

"Don't tell me, let me guess. There's a pack of wolves surrounding the truck. They have guns, and there's no way out."

"Are you sure you didn't hit *your* head?" he asked. "It's nothing like that. It's, well, we're both freezing. I think we would do better to share some body heat." He stared forward through the cracked front window while he spoke, sounding almost shy.

"Oh."

He turned to look at her then. "Oh? That's it? I thought you would scream and plunge from the car in a fit of rage or something."

"Maybe I would if I could feel my legs," she answered. "But you're probably right. Sharing body heat is the practical thing to do."

Still, neither of them made a move toward the other. They were strangers. Strangers who didn't much like each other, and she was dating his brother. The situation couldn't get much more awkward. She felt her cheeks heat with a blush, and for some reason she felt like crying all of a sudden. This wasn't the way her vacation was supposed to go. She should be with Cam right now, working up to a good night kiss. Instead, she was freezing to death with his surly twin and about to pass out from the mortification of having to cuddle with a stranger.

"Come on," Coy said gently. "Let's get it over with." He held out his arms to her.

She wrinkled her nose at him, even though he couldn't see her. "Don't sound so enthused." She scooted across the seat until she was close enough to touch him, then slowly eased herself into his stiff embrace.

"Don't tell me this is how you dreamed of spending your evening," he said. He closed his arms around her and she was relieved when the embrace felt platonic. If she could think of him like her brother she might survive the ordeal. With that thought in mind, she relaxed a little and rested her head on his shoulder after settling both their blankets around them.

"No, this is definitely not how I dreamed of spending my evening."

"How did you plan to spend it?" he asked curiously. "Did you and Cam have big plans? He didn't really say."

"I suppose we would have spent some time talking and getting to know each other in person."

He snorted a laugh as he tried to picture his brother unbending enough to go on a date.

"What's the laugh for?" she asked testily.

"How well do you know Cam?"

She frowned. "What's wrong with Cam?"

"Nothing." Now he sounded testy. "Cam is great. But he's not the hero in a romantic story book. He doesn't know how to relax and let his hair down."

"Maybe he needs someone to show him."

"I suppose," Coy said, although he didn't sound convinced. When he first saw her at the airport, he had been convinced she was a lifeless ice queen, incapable of feeling. She was exactly the sort of girl Cam would be attracted to, and exactly the sort of girl he shouldn't date. He should date someone strong-willed and passionate who might be able to ignite him out of his own coldness. Since the accident, he was seeing a whole new side of Ivy, and he thought she might be the sort of strong-willed, passionate girl Cam needed. But he still felt uncomfortable with the thought of her with Cam. Why, though?

"Is Ivy short for something?" he asked as a way to divert his uncomfortable thoughts.

"Yes it is," she murmured sleepily against his chest. "It's short for

'Call me Poison Ivy One More Time and I'll Rip Off Your Lips and Make You Eat Them.'"

He laughed, unconsciously drawing her closer as he did so. "That's a mouthful. I can see why you shortened it. Is it really short for something?"

"Ivandra," she murmured.

"Ivandra," he repeated. "That's pretty."

She grunted and he took that to mean she wasn't a fan of her given name. The warmth between them was spreading, making them sleepy. He yawned and settled more comfortably against the seat, taking her with him. She readjusted her position until she was comfortable, too, and sleep began to steal over them. He had barely enough energy left for one more whisper.

"Goodnight, Poison Ivy," he said, then chuckled when she pinched him hard in the stomach.

IVY SLEPT FITFULLY and woke early as the sun was coming up. Her body was warm, but her face was freezing. As she woke more fully she realized her face was the only part of her uncovered and not pressed against Coy. With dawning horror she discerned at some point in the night her arms had slipped around his waist and she was now clutching him tightly. Still, she was reluctant to let go. Holding on to him represented warmth; letting him go meant being cold. But with dawning awareness came the return of the awkwardness she had felt last night. Reluctantly, she let him go and eased away.

"You're awake," he said unnecessarily. He stared bleakly through the front windshield. She followed the line of his vision and bit back a gasp.

"It must have snowed at least six inches," she said.

"Eight by my calculation with ice underneath that."

She stared up at him, alerted by the despair in his tone. Already she understood he was the type of person who faced problems head on instead of mourning over them. For him to be upset meant there was more on his mind he wasn't telling her. "What are you thinking?"

"There's no way anyone can see us from the highway. Our tracks are covered. The truck is white. Even if they do an aerial search there's a good chance the truck will blend in with the snow."

"What are you saying?" she asked.

"I'm saying I don't think a rescue is coming. We're going to have to walk out of here."

"Walk." She repeated the word as if she had never heard it before.

"More like hike, really. There aren't any mountains, but I wouldn't say it's flat and easy going."

"Can't we walk on the road?" she asked.

He shook his head. "By the road it's a good thirty miles to home, and that's if we could climb up that ravine. It's still covered in ice. As the crow flies, it's less than twenty. There's a chance someone might be out driving looking for us, but with this weather, there's a good chance they won't. We're so remote the road crews leave us for last. There's no need to add ten miles to our hike if we don't have to."

Nervously, she licked her lips and stared through the front windshield. "And you know how to get home from here?"

"I could do it blindfolded. And it's twenty miles to the house. We'll reach our land sooner than that. There's a good chance we'll run into one of the ranch hands who can give us a ride back."

"How long will it take?"

"If we can do ten miles a day then it will take two days." He didn't tell her ten miles a day was optimism on his part. Ten miles on a horse was a long, difficult ride. Ten miles on foot would be exhausting, maybe impossible, especially with all the snow and ice. And he had no idea what her fitness or endurance level was. Still, he was hopeful they would be three days at the most. His stomach growled, reminding him of another, more pressing concern. What were they going to do for food and water? They had barely enough water for today, and no food. With as fast as they needed to move, there would be no time to hunt. Even if by some miracle he shot a rabbit or bird, how were they supposed to cook it? He had matches, but he wasn't naïve enough to believe he would be able to start a fire with wet wood and everything, everywhere was wet.

He blew out a breath, trying not to show how deeply concerned he really was. She was his responsibility until he got her home. Part of that responsibility included keeping her from being afraid.

While he was musing over all they would need to do, he realized she was leaning over the back seat, rifling through her bags. He hoped she wouldn't insist on trying to take all of her suitcases. She couldn't be that dumb, could she?

"We'll have to leave those here and come back for them with the tow truck," he told her.

She paused to give him a disdainful look. "I'm tucking the necessities into my backpack. I assume you'll want to have food, water, and other emergency supplies, won't you?"

At the mention of food, he perked up. "You have food in there?"

"A little," she admitted sheepishly. "I have low blood sugar. I always travel with snacks."

"What kind of snacks?"

"A few granola bars. And some chocolate."

Now it was his turn to sit up on his knees and lean over the seat. He was stiff and sore from sitting so long in one position. "Chocolate? Let me see." He caught her hand and moved it out of the way to reveal a large stash of dark chocolate candy.

He laughed and looked at her in surprise. "That's a whole lot of chocolate for one person."

"It's a two week trip. I wanted to make sure and have a steady supply. I eat chocolate when I'm nervous, okay?"

He glanced at the huge pile of chocolate. "You must have been planning to be really nervous."

She gave him a light shove. "Shut it or I won't share."

He sat down again, still smiling. "What else of value do you have in there?"

"A magazine to help start fires, extra socks, a tiny amount of water, and some wet wipes. Help me fold these blankets, and I'll stuff those in there, too. Are you sure you're able to travel with that head of yours?"

"I've gotten this far in life fine with it," he said.

"Yes, but previously it wasn't covered in blood and bruises." She paused and put her hand on his arm. "I need you to be honest with me about how you're doing. Please."

"I'm fine, really. The head aches, but it's nothing I can't handle. How about you? Are you up to some hiking today?"

"Do I have a choice?" she asked.

He smiled. "No, but I would prefer to know if it becomes too much for you."

"It won't be too much for me," she assured him.

He gave her a dubious look.

She drew herself up and scowled at him. "I'm an athlete. I'm in good condition."

"An athlete, huh? Competitive shopper?"

"Try starting point guard for the University of Kentucky women's basketball team, although I graduated last year and haven't played much since then. I still keep in shape."

She couldn't have surprised him more if she said she was an astronaut for NASA. "Basketball, no kidding?"

"I never kid about basketball," she told him.

"You don't look like a ball player," he said.

"Why, have all the players you've known had three arms or some other distinctive feature?"

He was about to say all the other female ball players he'd seen hadn't been nearly as pretty as she was, but he caught himself in time. "You didn't strike me as an athlete, that's all."

She supposed it was a compliment in a roundabout sort of way. Some female athletes looked like men. She had always prided herself on maintaining her femininity, especially in light of her testosterone-filled childhood. "Thank you, I think. Should we get this show on the road?" She gestured toward the front of the car.

"Let's warm up a bit and then go. We can have the remainder of our sodas for breakfast." He turned the ignition and started the truck. It made an unhealthy screeching sound but roared to life. He blasted the heat, and after a few minutes the chill started to seep from her bones.

Being warm was heavenly and she never wanted it to end. With a small sense of panic, she realized this might be the last time she was warm for several days. During the daylight, they would probably be okay. Temperatures would be cold, but not cold enough to freeze them. Nighttime was another story, though. How were they supposed to survive out in the elements when the thermometer dropped below zero as it undoubtedly had last night? And for that matter, wasn't there a lot of wildlife out here?

"When do grizzly bears hibernate?" She tried to ask it casually.

"November or so. But don't worry, we haven't had any grizzly problems for a while now. Not to say there aren't any around, but we probably won't run into any. And if we do, I have a gun." Not that his handgun would do much to take down a grizzly, but there was no need to tell her that.

"Is it a high-powered rifle?"

He looked at her in surprise, something he was beginning to do a lot. "No, it's a hand gun."

"So basically shooting one would be about as effective as throwing your gun at it?"

Should he placate her or be honest? "Pretty much." He grinned. "But it might be enough to scare one off."

She returned his smile. "So we're clear on things, we're about to take a twenty mile hike in the Montana wilderness in freezing temperatures with eight inches of snow on the ground when neither of us has a winter coat, hat, gloves, tent, food or water. Along with having no protection from the elements, we also have no protection from any wildlife we might encounter. Oh, and we've been in a bad car accident, are weak and sore, and you're covered in blood like a grizzly's dream appetizer. Did I miss anything?"

He rubbed his hand over his scratchy whiskers and pretended to think. "We do have one secret weapon you're forgetting about," he said.

"What's that?"

"If a grizzly gets near us, you can probably talk it to death."

"Keep in mind one very important thing, Mr. King," she said.

"What's that, Miss Honeywell?"

"I don't have to outrun a bear. I only have to outrun you, and, sugar, I can do that with one leg tied behind my back." She tossed him a little wink, dimpling when his expression closed in a mutinous frown.

CHAPTER 6

$\mathcal{C}$oy was not happy. In fact, he was downright angry. Ivy hadn't been exaggerating about being an athlete. And he wasn't prepared for the physical toll the accident had taken on him. Now she was the one setting the pace as he lagged behind. Even worse, she insisted on carrying the backpack. His head was killing him, he ached all over, and he was cold. He felt like an invalid, and it galled him to think a girl was doing more work than he was. And perhaps what was worst of all was that she was being *nice* about it. The least she could do was tease him about his weakened condition, but instead she stopped every twenty feet or so in order to "rest." In reality, they both knew she was giving him the chance to catch up with her.

Hiking through the snow over the rough terrain was as exhausting as he had thought it would be, but she showed no signs of slowing down. He was beginning to wonder if she was a robot. He was accustomed to working in all sorts of harsh weather conditions. He had been stranded outside a few times in cold, snowy weather, but never had he been this miserable. Granted, he was usually on his horse and better prepared for the weather. Now his clothing was grossly inadequate. He had tucked his jeans into his cowboy boots so they wouldn't get wet, but the cold was seeping through his boots, making his feet numb. He had never thought of himself as a complainer before, but he was quickly revising his opinion. He wanted a hot meal and a warm bed in that order. Ivy was keeping him stocked in pain reliever, but it was barely taking the edge off his headache. Every step seemed to compound his misery.

Now as she sat for another break, her third in an hour, he wanted to simultaneously weep with joy and shout with indignation that he didn't need to be coddled. Then she held out a piece of chocolate to him and he stumbled forward, reaching for it as he sat on a fallen log.

"How far do you think we've gone?" she asked.

He unwrapped the chocolate and popped it in his mouth before answering. "Maybe three miles."

Three miles? Could that really be it? They had been traveling for half the day already. Ivy felt shaky with hunger and exhaustion, and they hadn't even reached a third of their goal for the day. She took a sip of water and handed the bottle to him. They had decided to share their water so when one bottle emptied they could pack it with snow. They had already emptied the little bit she had leftover from the airplane. She had packed it with snow as soon as they finished drinking. She pulled it out now to check its progress.

What had started as a bottle full of snow was now a little over a quarter inch of water. With a sigh, she loaded the bottle with more snow—a tedious process by any means. But at least it would give Coy a chance to rest and hopefully restore some of his good humor. He had started out happy enough when they left the truck and almost immediately turned grumpy and sullen. *Stupid male pride,* she thought. After so much time spent with her brothers, she knew men didn't like to be beaten by women, and it had to be killing him that she was doing better with the hiking than he was. Of course he wouldn't take his head injury into consideration and give himself a break. No, instead he would take his bad mood out on her because she was beating him. One more example of why she couldn't wait to arrive at the ranch and see Cam. Maybe she owed Coy her life. That didn't mean she had to like him.

Coy watched Ivy load more snow into the nearly empty bottle. He would never have thought of that. The fact that she had was one more reason to both begrudge and admire her. In addition to putting herself in charge of their food supply, she had also combed her suitcases to search for anything else they might be able to use. She came up with a pair of waterproof jogging pants with an elastic waistband she had insisted he slip over his pants. The length was too short and they were slightly tight, but they covered most of his legs and made him significantly warmer. She was also wearing a pair of them over her jeans. He was far from comfortable, but he wasn't as miserable as he could have been, thanks to her.

She had tucked her hair back in its clip, but it didn't look as severe today. Or maybe it was the fact that he knew her better now and would never be able to think of her as severe again. Now he wondered how he could have ever thought of her as an ice princess in the first place. Sure, she told him off and put him in his place, but there was nothing icy about her. In fact, she was a little firecracker. He wondered where she got all her courage and determination. He wondered a lot of things about her. He was suddenly curious to know everything and, with as many hours as they had to pass together, why not spend some time talking?

"Do you have brothers or sisters?" he asked.

She closed her eyes and took a breath as if preparing herself for something unpleasant. "I have five older brothers."

Five older brothers? If he had a little sister as cute as she was, he would never let a guy get close to her. "How did they feel about your trip out here to see Cam?"

She looked up at him then, an angry, defiant expression on her face. "I didn't tell them."

"You didn't tell them? Are you crazy? You can't go off half-cocked across the country to meet some man you met on the internet without telling your family."

"I told my family. I made my parents promise not to tell my brothers."

"Why not?"

She sighed and sat back. "Because I didn't want to spend the rest of my life being teased about meeting a man on the internet. 'What's the matter, Ivy, couldn't you get anyone who actually knows you? Did you send him fake pictures so he wouldn't be turned off by your real face?'"

Despite his best intentions not to, he laughed. "But they're teasing you," he said.

"So they say."

"Why do you let them get to you? They're trying to get a rise out of you."

"Don't you think I know that?" she asked. "Don't you think my parents have been saying that for the past twenty two years? But that doesn't make it any easier to be the girl whose brothers stormed every sleepover I ever went to in order to perform a well-executed panty raid. And it doesn't make it any less embarrassing when my brothers elected themselves as the first all male cheerleading squad for the University of Kentucky's lady's basketball team. For four years I was known as the girl whose brothers donned matching cheerleading outfits and led the crowd in chants of 'Let's go wildcats!' It's not funny." She punched him lightly in the shoulder to try and stop his laughter, but then she started to giggle, too. "People started coming to my games to see them. For all four years I was on the team, we had record attendance." They laughed together for a few minutes before fatigue set in, making them too tired to do much more than sit.

"We should go before we lose all motivation," she said, peering at him from the corner of her eye. "Are you ready?"

"Ready," he said. It would have been rewarding to confirm that statement by jumping to his feet. Instead he lumbered slowly into a standing position like a frail, old man, then stood staring at her when she lightly touched his forearm.

"This is only temporary, you know. You're injured."

"I'm not used to being helpless," he said.

"You're not helpless. A little slow on the draw, maybe."

"I suppose," he said. He shuffled off in the direction of the house. Instead of resuming her normal pace, she remained walking beside him. After a few minutes, she reached over and slipped her hand in his, clasping tightly. It was amazing how that small spark of warmth and support encouraged him to keep putting one foot in front of the other.

They walked a few more hours until the sun started to fade. It was too much effort to talk, so they meandered in silence, each one trying to make as much progress as possible. Despite their determination, their steps became slower as the day progressed. Coy was sapped of energy because of his injury, and Ivy's blood sugar was low, making her weak and shaky.

"Are you going to pass out?" Coy asked in concern. She was pale and sweaty and her hand was trembling slightly in his.

"I'll be okay," she assured him. "Mostly it makes me grumpy to feel so bad."

"You? Grumpy? I won't believe it until I see it," he said sarcastically.

She stuck her tongue out at him, and he laughed.

"This looks like a good spot to make camp," he said, surveying the flat terrain. They were surrounded by several pine trees and boulders that formed a natural shelter around the site.

"This isn't really my area of expertise. What should we do first?" she asked.

"First we need to construct a shelter and we need to gather firewood, not necessarily in that order."

"Why don't you work on the shelter? I have a feeling I would be more of a liability. I'll see what I can do about gathering some wood."

He nodded absently as he mentally began planning a shelter. "Look for some pine sap. It makes a good fire starter."

"Will do," she said. She paused at the edge of the trees, intimidated by the darkness within, then she took a breath and plunged in. One last glance behind her showed Coy pulling out his pocket knife and then she set her mind on her task. The good thing about the density of the trees was not much snow had filtered down to the ground here. The wood would be damp, but not soaking wet. Right away she found a plethora of fallen twigs along with some hardened pine sap from an injured tree. Her good mood lasted until she began scraping the sap from the tree. All at once she realized the four stripes in the tree were most likely from a bear paw. She spread her hand out, trying to make it reach all four lines at once, but the size dwarfed her hand. It had to be a grizzly. No black bear was that big. With shaking fingers, she resumed her task.

She swallowed hard, picturing a grizzly hiding behind a tree and watching her like a deranged bear stalker. Then she laughed at herself for her stupidity. If there was a grizzly nearby, he would have no need to hide and watch her. He would know he would be the victor in any confrontation and therefore have no need for fear or stealth. She tried and failed to take comfort in that fact.

After gathering as many twigs and as much sap as she could hold, she returned to the campsite. The twigs were plentiful enough to make a few trips necessary and she had a large pile going, but they would go quickly once the fire started. What she needed were some large logs that would burn for a long time. A few minutes of searching revealed a couple of limbs the size of her arm, but they were too long. She dragged them to the campsite and used her foot to try and break them into pieces. After a few minutes of seeing her struggle with the largest portion of the branches, Coy moved her aside and used his boot to break the branch as if it were twigs. He was either too tired or too polite to tease her about his superior strength because when he finished breaking the logs he returned to his work without a word.

When her task was completed, she stood back to admire his shelter. It was rough, to be sure, and very small, but it looked sturdy enough to last the night and keep out the wind. He had banded a few long limbs together with wild grapevine and cut boughs from pine trees to drape over top. Thinking of the pine trees caused her to peer inside the shelter at the hard ground. While he finished constructing the shelter, she used his knife to cut some more pine branches to spread on the ground. It wasn't much, but anything that would provide a cushion between them and the cold, hard ground would be worth it.

As soon as that task was completed, she wanted to begin making the fire, but she didn't know how.

"How do you make a fire?" she asked Coy.

"Put your sap in the middle. Crumple up the magazines around it. Lay sticks overtop that, but don't compact them. Air is important." He tossed her the matches and smiled at her when she caught them. "Nice catch."

"Good throw," she said.

He laughed and turned his attention to finishing his job. She took her time arranging the fire. They had a book full of matches, but from previous attempts at building fires she knew how quickly matches could become depleted. Building a fire was a skill she didn't take for granted, especially when their survival depended on it.

When she was satisfied she had everything properly arranged, she struck the match and lit a crumpled piece of magazine. It caught and then burned through too quickly to light anything else. With a growl of frustration she tried again, silently praying this time it would catch. It didn't. By the third try, her patience had reached an end, but, thankfully, a twig caught, and then some of the pine sap. Ivy sat back, delighted but watchful. She had no intention of letting her fire die, but she didn't want to feed it too much and overwhelm it. She focused all her attention on gently adding twigs and arranging the pile until she felt a little more confident of the fire's sustainability.

"Hey, that looks good," Coy said, plopping down beside her. She was famished and parched, but she had waited on him to eat or drink anything. Now she fished out their water bottle and handed it to him. He took a swig and handed it back. Earlier in the day, they had finished off one of the water bottles and decided to save the second bottle for the next day. She had been diligent about refilling the bottles with snow, but even so there were only a few sips.

"We should reach our land sometime tomorrow," Coy told her. "I know where a stream is. It's a little out of the way, but if our water supply is low it will be worth it."

"Sounds good," she lied. Anything besides hot food and a soft warm bed sounded horrible, but saying so wouldn't help the situation any. "Want some chocolate?" She handed him a couple of pieces without waiting for an answer. They had eaten the bag of peanuts from the emergency kit at lunch, deciding to save the two granola bars for tomorrow's breakfast. There was still plenty of chocolate though had been snacking on it all day.

The sun had been out all day and the temperature had been pleasant, probably somewhere in the low fifties. The snow had started to melt, causing an icy slush that made walking more difficult, but at least it had been warm. But now as the sun started to dip, so did the temperature. Ivy shivered and drew closer to the fire, sticking out her hands and rubbing them together.

"You did great today, Ivy. Thanks for everything."

She stared at her hands in mute surprise. If it had been one of her brothers with her, he would no doubt have pointed out her many shortcomings during the day, teasing her about all the times she had lagged. Hearing a compliment from Coy was probably the last thing she expected. She was touched by his sweetness.

"Thanks, Coy. You did pretty great yourself."

He snorted in disgust. "Please. I was a liability."

She scowled at him. "Not true at all. Without you I wouldn't have a clue how to build a shelter or make a fire."

"You would have figured it out," he said confidently. "I slowed you down today. Without me, you could have made a few more miles of progress."

"No, I couldn't. I'm exhausted. I wanted to shout with joy when you said we were stopping here for the night. I'm not sure I could have taken one more step."

Now it was his turn to be surprised. She hadn't complained once the entire day. He had no idea she was tired. From all appearances, she was some sort of Sherpa for whom hiking came as naturally as breathing.

"You're not at all what I thought you were," he said.

"Since you pretty much hated me on sight, I'm assuming any revision in your opinion is a good thing."

He blushed, glad she couldn't see it. "I'm sorry about that. I guess

I'm a little protective of Cam. He's not always the most sensible when it comes to girls. He hasn't had a lot of experience."

"Really?" she asked in surprise. "But he's so handsome."

He frowned, not sure why it should bother him to have her describe his brother as handsome. He was her boyfriend, after all. "The ranch is remote. We don't have much contact with girls."

She laughed. "Something tells me that hasn't been a problem for you."

He smiled. "Not hardly." He had dated more than his share of girls. If you knew where to look, finding one wasn't a problem. His smile changed to a frown. Finding one had never been a problem. Keeping one was another story. Ever since Cade and Layla became serious, he had been thinking about things that never occurred to him before. He was almost twenty two years old and had never had more than a temporary flirtation with anyone. Previously, he had never wanted to. But after seeing the loving depth between Layla and Cade things changed. Lately, he had been feeling a new kind of emptiness he didn't know existed before. He supposed Cam had been feeling the same thing, and maybe that was why he had uncharacteristically reached out to Ivy.

"I've lost you," she said.

"I was thinking deep thoughts. Doesn't happen often, so it caught me by surprise."

"Do you have a girlfriend?"

"No."

"Why not?"

He shrugged.

"Don't you want a girlfriend?"

"I suppose." How had they gotten on this uncomfortable topic?

"Then why don't you have one?"

"I don't know. Are you in the CIA, or something?" he snapped.

"Touchy," she drawled.

He took a deep breath, trying to stifle his irritation. "What about you, have you dated much before Cam?"

"No." Her tone was clipped.

"Why not?"

"Five older brothers."

"What does that have to do with anything?"

"If you met them, you'd know," she said. "Why do you think I had to meet a man in secret on the internet and fly halfway across the country to get to him?" Angrily, she tossed another stick on the fire.

A change of topic seemed like a good idea. Clearly, she had some issues with her brothers. "What do you do for a living?"

"Cam didn't tell you?"

He shook his head.

She smiled. "You're right; Cam is good at keeping secrets. My family breeds horses. I'm in the family business."

His jaw dropped. "You're a breeder?"

"*Horse* breeder," she said. "You made me sound like one of those people who has a million kids."

He snorted a laugh. "So you can actually ride a horse."

"Generally, when one breeds horses, it's a good idea to know how to ride them. I've been riding horses since the day I was born. And that's not an exaggeration. My oldest brother snuck me out of the house, jumped into the saddle and took me on a ride three hours after I was born."

"You're kidding me," he said.

"I'm not. You think I'm exaggerating about my brothers. I'm not. If anything, I'm editing the gory details for you. It's a wonder I survived my childhood." She paused to sigh before continuing again. "Cam wants me to take a look at your horses while I'm here. He said if..." She broke off and stared at the fire.

"He said what?" he asked. Cam tended to run the ranch like a one man operation. If he was making a business decision that involved Ivy, Coy wanted to know about it.

"He said if things work out between us, he might consider having me run a breeding operation out here. He thinks it would be a lucrative addition to the ranch," she finished shyly. To her embarrassment, Coy began to laugh. "What? What is it?"

He shook his head and tried to rein in his laughter. "It's Cam. Here

I am thinking he's gone off the deep end for some girl, and it turns out the whole thing is a business deal. Now everything makes sense." He was still so caught up in his own amusement it took him a minute to realize she jumped up and strode away from the fire.

"Now I've stuck my foot in it," he muttered.

* * *

IVY HAD NEVER BEEN MORE angry, hurt, and confused in her life. All her insecurities over Cam's interest in her rose to the surface and threatened to overwhelm her. All along, a little voice in the back of her head had been telling her it was too good to be true a handsome, successful, wealthy rancher was interested in her for her. She should have known it wasn't her he wanted. Just her knowledge of horses, and her family's connections. She thought Montana was too far for her family name to carry any weight in the horse world. She should have known better. While she had been picturing fairytales and sunsets, Cameron King had apparently been picturing money and burgeoning empires.

"Stupid," she muttered. She wanted to stomp around the lean-to until she relieved some of her pent up anger, but that would no doubt destroy the shoddy structure, precarious as it was. Instead she contented herself with lying stiffly on the hard ground. When Coy entered the shelter a few minutes later, she rolled over on her side away from him and jerked the blankets up to her chin.

He lay down in silence a few inches away from her. He didn't reach for the blankets. She felt a little guilty over that because it was freezing, but she was too angry to offer him anything.

Coy's stomach was twisting with guilt. Somehow he had upset Ivy, and he had to make it right, even if he didn't know how. "Ivy," he whispered. There was no answer, even though he knew she was still awake. He sat up and leaned over her, and then he saw it—the telltale glimmer of tears in her eyes.

"I made you cry," he breathed in a dazed sort of way. He felt like someone had slammed a fist in his gut, taking all his air.

"Did not," she said as she swiped furiously at her eyes.

"Please don't cry, please. I didn't mean it. You misunderstood me."

"Misunderstood?" she repeated angrily. She twisted around so her back was on the ground and she was looking up at him. "How could I misunderstand that Cam is only interested in me for my knowledge of horses?"

He laughed, but the sound was more desperate than amused. "Ivy, this is Montana. Sparsely populated as it is, you could still throw a stick and hit someone who knows about breeding horses. Believe me when I tell you that's not why he's interested in you. But I know my twin. He is shy and reserved. I've been wracking my brain trying to figure out how he got up the courage to talk to a pretty girl, much less ask her to spend two weeks with him. But if you have a business connection it makes sense. He would have used that to his advantage."

She blinked up at him, sniffling in startled surprise. "You...you think I'm pretty?"

The fist of tension in his stomach melted until it felt like molten lava spreading through him all the way to his fingers and toes. One of those fingers reached out now, brushing a silky tendril of hair at her temple. "I think you're about the prettiest thing I've ever laid eyes on," he said softly.

"Oh." She blinked up at him, her tear-wet lashes and swollen, puffy lips doing nothing to detract from the beauty of her face. It was amazing to him she didn't understand how attractive she was.

"Did your brothers tell you you're not pretty?" he guessed. It was the only possible way she couldn't know.

"They told me I'm the runt of the litter and my parents only kept me because I'm a girl."

His fists clenched at his sides. He was really beginning to dislike these brothers of hers. "I'd like to have a few minutes alone with each of your brothers."

For some reason she found that really funny. She giggled, hiccupped, and wiped her eyes. "Thanks, Coy. I'm sorry I'm so emotional. It's the low blood sugar."

And the all day hike, and the uncertainty of their situation, and any other number of factors that would cause any other woman to sit down and give up. But Ivy hadn't given up. She hadn't even complained.

"Come here," he said gently. He held out his arms to her and she curled toward him, burrowing her face against his shirt. "Let's get some sleep. Everything will seem better in the morning." His hand made a soothing pass over her back. With effort, he resisted the urge to kiss the top of her head, especially when she burrowed closer, nestling.

"Best idea I've heard all day," she muttered sleepily. She arranged the blankets to cover both of them, and then she fell asleep.

Coy wasn't so lucky, though. He lay awake a long time trying to puzzle over his wayward emotions.

CHAPTER 7

The next morning Ivy woke with an odd sense of amnesia. There was a reason she was stiff and sore, but she couldn't figure out what it was. Beneath her was cold, hard, and damp, and yet she was almost toasty warm. But why?

Remembrance came with a jolt. She was spooning. With Coy. They were fitted tightly together with her back to his front. His arm was draped over her and curled protectively. All in all, she felt very cozy, and that in itself was enough to disturb her from any further thoughts of sleep.

Her face flushed with guilt. Should she be so comfortable curled up next to her boyfriend's brother? What would Cam say if he knew how close she and Coy had been during the night? Then again, it's not as if they had any choice. Sharing body heat was a necessity. They hadn't started out spooning. At some time in the night their bodies must have gone in search of heat and comfort and found this position. Cam would understand basic survival instincts, wouldn't he?

"Are you awake?" Coy whispered, his breath warm on her ear.

"Yes," she whispered.

Neither of them moved.

"Did you sleep?" he asked after a pause.

"I did," she replied. "I didn't think I would."

"Exhaustion took over. We expended a lot of energy yesterday."

"How's the head?"

"Better," he said, sounding relieved. He hoped he would be able to pull his weight today. "Do you want to eat breakfast now or walk awhile first?"

Her heart sank at the thought of the one meager granola bar she would be able to eat that day.

"Walk awhile, I guess."

"That's what I was thinking, too. We should probably get started soon."

Still, neither of them made a move to leave the shelter. There were physiological reasons human touch was soothing. Plenty of articles had been written about how it lowered blood pressure, slowed the heart rate, and eased physical pain. Right now none of those articles came to mind. Ivy only knew lying there, being held by Coy, was intensely comforting. She had no desire to change the status quo.

"I fed the fire a few times in the night, but we ran out of wood. The coals might give off some warmth still."

She twisted in order to see his face. "You fed the fire in the night? I didn't hear you."

"You were pretty out of it." He propped himself on one elbow and smiled down at her.

He had a dimple. She wondered how she had missed it because, as dimples went, it was a deep one. Even his two days worth of stubbly growth did nothing to disguise it. She probably hadn't noticed it before because she hadn't really looked closely at him. Now that she did, she realized he was very handsome.

There was enough resemblance between him and Cam to denote relation, but not enough to tell they were twins. For one thing, Cam didn't have a dimple. At least, she didn't think so. As she thought back over pictures she had seen and their webcam chats, she couldn't ever remember seeing him laugh. Hmm, strange. He had given her a few, tentative smiles, but that was it.

In addition to lack of a dimple, Cam's hair was a lighter shade of brown, almost blond. It was cropped close to his head in a crew cut. Coy's hair was sandy brown with gold streaks and long enough to curl at the ends, especially around his ears.

"Does Cam ever laugh?" she blurted.

Coy's smile slipped and his expression closed up. "Sometimes. Not often. We should get this show on the road." He stood and exited the enclosure, leaving an icy emptiness in his wake.

They walked for an hour before stopping. They each ate a half a granola bar and drank a few sips of water, trying desperately to ignore the gnawing ache in their empty bellies. Coy was doing much better at keeping up today. The snow wasn't as deep as it had been. Now their only enemy was the rough terrain. If they were walking on a flat level surface they would no doubt be home by nightfall. As it was, he was convinced they would have to make camp one more night.

"I was thinking about pine trees," he said. "I heard once every part of a pine tree is edible. Maybe we should try chewing on some pine needles. I don't think they'll taste good, but I think they have a lot of vitamin C."

"At this point anything sounds good."

They stopped at the next pine tree they spotted, plucked some needles, and shoved them in their mouths.

"Taste like floor cleaner," she said, grimacing.

"No argument here."

They didn't spit them out, though. They didn't taste great, but they were something to chew on and they kept the horrible dry mouth feeling at bay.

"What about pine nuts?" she suggested.

"Never heard of them," he replied.

"They're used in fancy cooking. I think they actually come from pine cones, though."

"Hmm." He picked up a pine cone without breaking stride and began breaking it apart as he walked.

"What kind of pine tree is that?" It was different than any she had ever seen in Kentucky.

"It's a limber pine," he said absently. "This cone is empty. Maybe you have to pick them directly from the tree." He paused, retraced his steps, and searched the tree until he found a cone still hanging. Using his knife to cut it off the tree, he tossed it to her. "Sticky," he said.

She caught it and frowned at the sap now covering her fingers. He cut off a few more cones, stuffed his pockets with the extras, and began to pick at the one in his hand as they resumed walking.

She began to pick at hers, too. At the very least it gave her something to concentrate on other than her hunger, the cold, and her aching body. "Aha," she said as soon as she pried open a piece of the cone. A large seed fell out. Only after she put it in her mouth did she realize it had a hull on it. She bit the hull in two and spit it out like a sunflower seed. Coy found his own nut a few seconds later and did the same thing.

"They would taste better roasted with some salt, but they're really not bad. Good idea."

She wasn't used to being praised for her ideas. She sort of liked the warm glow of pleasure his words brought her. They walked in companionable silence as they picked at the pine cones. It wasn't easy to get the nuts out of the cones, but it helped to pass the time and also helped stave off the gnawing hunger, at least a little bit.

"I bet these have a lot of protein," she said. Protein would maintain their energy longer than the small infusions of chocolate they had been eating. The pine trees were plentiful, and she felt a little more enthusiastic about their situation. Maybe it wasn't ideal, but they wouldn't starve.

After they paused for a lunch that consisted of pine nuts, chocolate, and a gulp of water, Coy told her they were only a few miles from their land.

"If we push ourselves, we can make it to a sort of permanent campsite. We built a few emergency shelters around the edges of our property in case the weather ever catches us unaware."

"What do you mean by 'push ourselves'?" she asked warily.

"We're not going to be able to stop again, and we probably won't reach the sight until after nightfall. But there's a stream nearby, some firewood, and we won't have to build a shelter."

She jumped to her feet. "What are we waiting for? Let's go." She turned and took off like a shot, despite the fact that she had no idea where she was going.

He smiled at her retreating backside. She was a trouper, and he liked that about her. If he were being honest, he would admit there were a lot of things he liked about her. Namely, the way she fit perfectly in his arms when they slept. Realizing the direction his thoughts were heading, he clamped his lips together with determination. She was Cam's girl, not his. Just because this experience had formed some sort of bond between them didn't mean anything. Of course he would be attracted to her. Forced togetherness had that effect. Tomorrow they would return to the ranch and everything would settle back to normal. She would be with Cam and he…well, he would be alone. Again. Like always.

With a sigh of resignation, he stood to his feet and trailed after Ivy.

CHAPTER 8

They stumbled into the campsite a half hour after sundown, which was about two hours after their energy gave out. Despite the addition of pine nuts into their diet, they were exhausted, hungry, and thirsty. They had kept going only by clasping hands and pulling each other forward one step at a time. A couple of times she had stumbled and would have fallen if he hadn't caught her and dragged her to her feet again. The last twenty minutes, he had been fully supporting her with his arm around her waist.

After practically falling into camp, they were reluctant to move again, but they knew they had to. A fire would make the night much more comfortable and they needed water. Ivy could hear a stream babbling nearby and the sound brought the sting of tears to her eyes. Or it would have if she had any tears to spare. She didn't realize how dehydrated she was until her tears refused to come. At that point she realized water was a necessity and not a luxury.

"I'll get the water while you work on the fire," she told him. She crawled to her knees and felt around in the bag until she located both water bottles. Clutching them to her, she tried to pull herself to a standing position. After a few failed attempts, she sat still and tried to rally her energy.

"I'll get the water and build the fire," Coy said. He sounded only slightly more energetic than she had.

"No, I'll get the water. I can do it. Give me a minute." Despite her brave words, she couldn't seem to garner the strength needed to stand up.

Coy stood, put his arms down, and pulled her up. He rested his forehead on hers and closed his eyes. "Be careful in the woods. Go slowly. The terrain is rocky, especially near the water. It's not deep, but it wouldn't do for you to get wet right now."

"Okay," she whispered. "Thanks for the lift."

He smiled and pressed a kiss to her forehead before letting her go. "Sure thing, sugar," he murmured, mimicking her drawl. The spark of warmth spread from the spot on her forehead to the rest of her, giving her the energy she needed to head toward the woods. *Don't waste energy blushing,* she told herself. *It was an encouraging kiss on the forehead. No big deal.* At any other time she might not have listened to her inner monologue, but she was too exhausted to do anything else but shut off her emotions and focus on what needed to be done. Right now that consisted of putting one foot carefully in front of the other. Coy hadn't been exaggerating about the rough terrain. The soil was loose and rocky. She had to creep very slowly because the moon didn't provide enough light to illuminate a path. Thankfully, the abundance of rocks caused the stream to burble loudly as the water hit them. She might not be able to see where she was going, but she could hear the water and had no trouble finding it.

After what seemed like forever, she reached the stream's edge, knelt, filled the bottle and began gulping almost before she brought it to her lips. There was sand and grit in it, but she didn't care. Nothing had ever tasted so good in her life. She would have kept drinking forever except she knew Coy had to be as thirsty as she was. After draining one bottle of water, she refilled both of them, capped them, and turned around. And then she stopped short.

While the sound of the water had so clearly provided direction for her, there was no sound coming from the opposite direction to tell her where to go. "Coy," she called, but she knew her voice was drowned by the gurgling of the water.

She took a few tentative steps away from the stream and tried again. "Coy."

Nothing but silence greeted her.

She swallowed down a lump of rising panic. The stream hadn't been more than fifty feet from the campsite. He had to be around here somewhere. But what if he wasn't? What if he fell and hit his head or passed out from hunger? What if she was all alone? She had no idea where she was. How would she find help for him? What if he had been attacked by a bear?

No, she quickly discounted that idea. She definitely would have heard a bear attack, stream or no stream. She took a few more steps and called his name again. Again she was greeted by silence.

Thanks to the massive amount of water she had consumed she could now produce tears, and produce them she did, by the bucket. Suddenly everything felt like too much. She was too tired, too hungry, too weak, and too afraid. She wanted to go home to Kentucky. Most of all right now she wanted to find Coy.

As she was about to have an all out meltdown and scream his name, she saw the tiny flicker of a flame. Sobbing now, she ran toward the light, scrambling over the jutted rocks that lined her path. If she fell, she would be in real trouble, but she didn't care. All she cared about right now was reaching Coy and the safety and security he offered.

* * *

COY HAD BARELY GOTTEN the fire started when he heard a sound that froze his heart in fear. Ivy was crying. And not mere crying, but sobbing. He turned to see her dim outline barreling toward him, stumbling over everything in her path. By the time he realized she was upset he took out running for her, but it was too late. She had reached him.

Instinctively, he held out his arms to her, and she fell into them. He wrapped his arms around her and pulled her tight against his chest, making unintelligible soothing noises as he did so. She was shaking so hard her teeth rattled, trembling violently from head to foot.

"Ivy, what's wrong?" He had to ask it a few times before his voice registered enough for her to answer. "Sweetheart, what?"

"I couldn't find you," she said.

"I'm right here," he told her, but it did nothing to ease her hysterics. He sat and pulled her into his lap. Keeping one arm firmly around her, he leaned over to feed the fledgling fire. Then he wrapped both arms tightly around her and started to rock back and forth. Eventually her crying gave way to sniffles and hiccups.

"I brought you some water," she said at last. She sounded so tired his heart lurched. She tried to fish around in her pockets, but he pushed her hands aside and retrieved the water for himself. She watched while he unscrewed the water with one hand and drained an entire bottle, as she had done. When he was finished, he opened the other bottle and held it out to her, but she shook her head.

"You should drink some more. You lost a lot of water with those tears," he said. She didn't protest as he held the bottle to her lips, but she only took a few tiny sips.

"I'm all right," she whispered, but she didn't move away from him. Instead, she circled his neck with her arms, pressed her face to the hollow of his throat, and promptly fell asleep.

IVY WOKE in the shelter of the lean-to and immediately felt guilty. She hadn't walked here under her own steam. Exhausted as he was, Coy had carried her to this place last night. She stared at the ceiling, recriminating herself for being such a craven coward. Why had she let a little darkness cause her such panic? Coy must think she was an idiot.

She frowned. Why was she facing the ceiling? And where was Coy? Strange how in two short days she had grown accustomed to him sleeping beside her. Now the space felt empty. A little of her anxiety from the night before returned. But as she sat up, he stepped back into the shelter.

"Sorry, I was adding the last of the wood to the fire. I hope I didn't wake you."

"You didn't wake me," she assured him. Rather, it was the absence of his presence that woke her. He lay down beside her and raised his arm as if he were going to drape it around her. Then he thought better of that idea and let it fall limply between them. He rolled over on his back and stared at the ceiling, too, a few inches away. Then he took a deep breath and let it out slowly.

"Today's the day we reach home," he said.

"Today's the day," she echoed dully. She was too tired to understand her mixture of emotions. She should be elated this ordeal would soon be over, shouldn't she? Why was there a little grief mixed in with her relief?

Coy's hand inched toward her until his fingers were lightly brushing hers. She turned her hand toward him, and he wove their fingers together. She tilted her head until it rested on his shoulder.

"Ivy."

"Hmm."

"I'm sorry about before, in the beginning. I judged you unfairly, thought you were someone you aren't. I'm not usually like that, but everything back home feels like it's changing. I guess I don't do change well."

"It was partly my fault," Ivy hastened to say. "I spent a lot of years honing that frosty, unaffected persona."

"Because of your brothers?" he guessed.

"Because of my brothers who loved nothing better than to get a rise out of me, and because of the Honeywell name."

"How so?"

She wasn't certain how to say it without coming off exalted. "I'm from a small town. Our family has been in existence a while. People think…people assume…well, my family is, uh, well established," she said, shifting uncomfortably, hoping he would read between the lines without making her say it, and he did.

"Your family is loaded," he blurted.

She chuckled. "I suppose you could say that. We go back a ways."

"I get it," Coy said, and he did. Their family was the same in their small town: founders, established, moneyed. Theirs was the largest ranch in a massive area, and it had brought them a certain amount of stature. And something else, too. "Even though it's a blessing, it doesn't come without strings. Sometimes it feels a little like, well, a little like..."

"Prison," they said together and glanced at each other, sharing a sympathetic smile. Neither was complaining; both knew they were privileged and blessed beyond measure. But that didn't mean their lives were perfect, as people sometimes assumed they were. All his life people had watched Coy with a combination of envy and expectation he found cloying, to say the least. Knowing she understood that same feeling went a long way toward strengthening their growing bond.

"I'm glad I got to know you, Ivandra," Coy said tenderly, giving her a sweet, heartfelt smile. "I can't think of anyone who could have handled this situation better."

She sniffled, blinking furiously a few times. "Don't make me cry here, King."

He squeezed her hand. "Sorry."

They lay in comfortable silence another minute before she spoke again. "Coy."

"Hmm."

"The feeling is mutual."

He felt her smile against his shoulder, and he smiled too. Suddenly, he was faced with the overwhelming desire to kiss her. *This is your last chance,* he told himself. *In a few hours, you'll have to hand her over to Cam.* At the thought of his brother, he came back to reality. No matter what had passed between them, she was Cam's girl, not his. No matter how much he might now wish she was his, she wasn't.

She rested her free hand on his bicep, turned toward him, and curled into the fetal position. He turned toward her, mimicking her position so they were facing each other. Their hands were still clasped and resting between them. They shared a smile. Her blinks grew longer until suddenly she was asleep.

Coy resisted the almost overpowering urge to reach out and brush a lock of hair off her face. If she were free, if she weren't with his brother, how would things have been different between them? *I would definitely touch her more,* he thought, smiling wryly. He would have no compunctions about sweeping her hair off her face, gathering her close in his embrace, and kissing her.

His mind ran on a tangent for a few minutes as he imagined kissing Ivy. With a jolt, he realized the direction of his thoughts and worked to get them back under control. What was wrong with him? There had never been any rivalry between him and Cam. Why now did Coy feel resentful of what Cam had? Why was there a part of him that imagined stealing Ivy away from his brother? He frowned, feeling sick and ashamed. If it had been Cade before the accident, Coy might have given it a try. There had been times in the past where he and Cade had taken each other's girl because it had all been part of a fun competition.

But Cam had never been included in those events. His personality was solid and serious, not the type to easily woo and then lose a girl. If Coy even attempted to take Ivy away from him, Cam could be irreparably damaged, and so would their close relationship. Was it worth it? Was any girl worth that? *Yes.* NO! He squinched his eyes shut, trying to block out the warring, traitorous thoughts. Loyalty and honor were traits branded into all the brothers since birth. Coy wouldn't be the first King to break with tradition and put his own needs and wants ahead of those of his family.

Besides, he was being presumptuous. Ivy had made clear she was here for Cam, hadn't she? Because their time together had somehow caused a warming trend in their relationship didn't mean she was on the same plane he was. The attraction he felt was probably all one-sided. But what if it wasn't?

On and on his thought tumbled while Ivy slept, her hand occasionally twitching ever so slightly in his. He smiled and, before he realized what he was doing, his free hand short-circuited his brain and began gently brushing her hair off her forehead as he had previously wanted to do. But even when he came to his senses, he didn't stop. The comforting motion caused her to fall into a deeper sleep. The tremors in her hand died out, and her breathing became deeper.

Even in sleep she was lovely. Eventually Coy's hand became tired of running gently over her head, but he lacked the willpower to pull it away. Instead he left it lying on the side of her face, cupping her cheek, his fingers tangled loosely in her hair. It was the perfect kissing arrangement; his hand was at the right angle to pull her closer and tip her face up to his. The thought sent his heart thudding painfully, but of course he didn't kiss her. Instead, he contented himself with studying her face, absorbing her beauty, and memorizing her features.

They had a long hike ahead of them. They needed to go. He should wake her. But he didn't. He lay still, listening to her gentle, even breathing and trying not to think this was the happiest he had ever been.

CHAPTER 9

They set off in silence hand in hand, too tired for conversation. The edges of Ivy's mind felt blurry, which was probably a good thing because it meant she couldn't concentrate on how horrible she felt. It wasn't that she was hungry, or thirsty, or tired, or dirty, or sore, or frazzled—it was all of it together. The combined misery was almost too much. If she had been alone, no doubt she would have thrown in the towel. But Coy's presence provided her the strength and stability she needed to keep going.

Thanks to the stream, they had plenty of water to start out with. They had no food and were too tired to hunt for pinecones. Instead they chose to concentrate what little energy they had into walking. Still, their breaks were becoming longer and more frequent as the morning wore on.

At about noon, Coy stopped short and put his arm around Ivy to stop her, too.

"Am I having a hallucination?"

She followed the line of his gaze and stared dumbfounded at a rider on a horse. "Only if I'm having it, too," she said.

"Hey!" He began calling to the man and waving his arms over his head, but the rider was too far away and facing the wrong direction.

Ivy stuck two fingers in her mouth and gave a piercing whistle that caused Coy to jerk away from her in surprise before covering his ear.

"Sorry, I should have warned you that was going to be loud," she said.

"What?" he asked, shaking his ear. But he was grinning as he turned toward the rider. His grin grew when the man reined in his horse and turned toward them. "It's Tanner," he said happily.

She was too tired to ask or care who Tanner was. All she knew was help had arrived.

"Coy," Tanner said as he drew closer. Although all the brothers were equal partners, their ranch hands only called Cam "boss." The rest of the brothers were called by their names.

"Hey, Tanner," Coy said tiredly.

"Everybody's been going haywire looking for you," Tanner said. He stared at Coy as if he were an apparition, and then did a double take when he saw Ivy.

"This is Ivy Honeywell, our guest."

"So far I've found Montana hospitality lacking," Ivy said, causing Coy to laugh.

"We'll see if we can do better from here on out," Coy said. He put his arm around her shoulders. "Can we borrow your horse?" he asked Tanner.

And like that, they were saved. Coy thanked Tanner and told him they would send a truck for him. Tanner smiled and pulled out a paperback western before propping himself on a fallen tree.

"Take your time," he said, waving them toward the horse.

Ivy stared at the horse, looking concerned.

"The saddle is big enough for both of us," Coy assured her.

"Of course it is. It's a western saddle. You could probably fit a couch up there."

He rolled his eyes. "Somehow I could have guessed you ride English."

She smiled at him distractedly and slid her hand down the horse's shoulder. "This horse is injured."

"What?" he asked, staring at the horse. It looked fine to him.

"See how he's standing? His weight is shifted to his right. I think he's, ah, right here. He has a contusion. Are any of the horses in your herd kickers?"

"Occasionally," he said. "Look, Ivy, I appreciate your concern for the horse, but right now my concern is for you. Let's go." He made a cradle of his hands and held them beside the horse.

She ignored his hands and easily vaulted into the saddle. He put his foot in the stirrup and settled in behind her.

"For the record, under normal circumstances I would never approve of riding an injured horse," she said.

"Duly noted," he replied.

"When we get back, someone needs to put an ice pack on that and he needs to stay off duty for a couple of days. Bruises like that can lead to bigger problems."

"Yes, ma'am," he said.

"You're humoring me so I'll shut up, aren't you?" she asked.

"With every fiber of my being."

She paused for a few beats. "Okay," she said, then leaned back against his chest and closed her eyes.

Even though their rescue had revived some of their energy, they still didn't talk on the ride back to the ranch. Ivy contented herself by watching the scenery. She was sure she hadn't ever seen anything more beautiful.

Coy contented himself by watching her. She was a mess. Dust and grime coated every surface of her body. She wore dirty, mismatched layers of clothing. Her hair had slipped from its confines and was tangled and matted all around her head. She wore no makeup and she didn't smell too great, either. He was sure he hadn't ever seen anything more beautiful. With every mile closer to home, his heart grew heavier. In a few minutes he would have to let go of her forever.

Rational thought told him they had only spent three days together. True, their time had been harrowing and had forced a bond between them. But he would get over her. He was pretty certain he would, anyway. At least, he hoped so. But he wouldn't get over her until she went away, and she wouldn't be going away for another week and a half. Until then he would have to watch her with his brother and try not to eat his heart out.

He sighed. Maybe he could go get lost in the wilderness again until she was gone. But the thought of being away from her, even if it was only for pretend, made his heart hurt. He had become accustomed to every expression, every sound, and every touch from her. How was he supposed to undo that?

And then, all too soon, they were home. There were several strange trucks in the yard. Coy guessed they were the search party. Their old hound dog began barking as he did whenever a cowboy returned from pasture. One of their hands looked up absently and then did a double take as he realized there were two riders on the horse and one of them was a girl. Immediately they were surrounded by a bevy of noise and activity. Ivy instinctively shied away from the crowd and toward Coy. As familiar as his friends and neighbors were to him, they were strangers to her.

Then Cam exited the barn and came toward them, his stride purposeful and unhurried as always. Coy and Ivy both tensed at the sight of him. The sun was behind them. He shaded his eyes, but probably couldn't see them, even though he squinted. The closer he got, though, the more tense Coy became. He had thought it would pain him to see the light of love and affection in Cam's eyes when he looked at Ivy. Nothing prepared him to feel angry towards his brother. But maybe his anger was due to the fact that there was no love light in Cam's eyes. There was only disappointment.

To Cam's credit, he immediately wiped his expression clean before pasting on a smile. But Ivy felt his initial reaction. Coy could tell by the slight hunching of her shoulders. Without allowing himself to think about it, he rested his hand on her waist and gave it a light squeeze.

"You've been holding out on me, Cam. You didn't tell me Ivy was some sort of expert horsewoman." Ivy blushed as the group of men turned to look at her with interest. "She could tell by looking this horse is injured."

Ivy's attention turned to the horse. "He has a contusion," she told

Cam. Coy was surprised to hear the shyness and reserve in her tone, but then he realized this was their first face to face meeting. "Can someone take care of him?" She gave the horse's neck a gentle pat.

"I'll see to it," Cam said. He put his arms up for Ivy, pulling her down off the horse before turning his attention to his brother.

"You don't look good."

"You're saying that because we're fraternal," Coy said, causing the group of men and Ivy to laugh. He swung down off the horse and handed the reins to one of their ranch hands. "Someone needs to get Tanner, and we'll have to call a tow about the truck. I'm pretty sure it's totaled."

Cam nodded and Coy knew he was making mental notes about what needed to be done, and also how much it would cost. Normally he didn't begrudge his brother his business sense; one of them had to keep things running smoothly. But right now he wished Cam would forget business and ask Ivy how she was doing. Other than giving her a cursory glance, he hadn't said much. Did she know that was how he was? Were her feelings hurt?

He sighed as he ran a weary hand over his scratchy whiskers. At this rate, he wasn't going to make it for the remainder of her visit. He had to stop acting like a lovesick schoolboy and let go of the situation. Ivy would have to figure out for herself his brother was more concerned with numbers than people.

"Are you okay, Coy?"

This came from Ivy who had stopped walking and was now looking at him with a pensive, worried expression. He stopped short, too, struck again by her beauty that couldn't be hidden even when she was covered in dirt.

"I'm fine," he lied.

Yes, it was going to be a very long week and a half, indeed.

CHAPTER 10

Their housekeeper, Layla, met them on the front porch. It was difficult for any of them to think of her as their house-keeper; she was more like family. Not only was she Cade's girlfriend, but she had lived with them for so long now no one remembered when she hadn't been there. She was funny and sweet and universally well liked by all the brothers, even Josh who was moody and stand-offish on the best of days.

"Oh my goodness," she gushed now, rushing forward to hug Coy tightly around the neck. "We were so worried."

He returned her hug before letting her go. They both turned toward Cam and Ivy, waiting for Cam to make the introductions.

"Layla Smith, this is Ivy Honeywell," Cam said.

"I know who she is," Layla said. She went forward and took Ivy's hands in both hers. "I'm so sorry for all that's happened to you. You must be starving and exhausted. Come with me, and I'll get you cleaned up. You can borrow some of my things until I wash and dry your clothes."

"Layla," Ivy said gently. Coy froze. Surely she wasn't going to refuse Layla's hospitality, was she?

"What?" Layla asked warily.

"I love you," Ivy said earnestly.

Layla chuckled as she led Ivy into the house behind her. "I have a feeling I'm going to feel the same way about you soon."

Coy smiled as he watched them walk into the house. "That went well," he said. One of his concerns in bringing Ivy here was that Layla might feel put upon. Except for their mother's occasional visits, Layla had been the only girl for a long time.

"Hmm," Cam said. "So what happened?"

"There was a bull moose in the road. Biggest one I've ever seen. We would have died if I hit it head on. I tried to go around it, but the roads were icy and we plummeted over a ravine."

Cam blew out a breath. "I'm not sure how that's going to go down with our insurance. If you had hit the thing our rates wouldn't go up, but since you swerved…" He let the thought trail off.

"Next time I'll make sure and die so your rates will stay really low," Coy said angrily.

Cam looked at him in surprise. If there was one thing Coy was, it was easygoing. He rarely said a cross word.

"Sorry," Coy apologized. "As you can imagine, it's been a rough few days."

Cam nodded. "Glad you're okay," he said. "I'd better make some calls."

Coy watched him go and tried to reel in his wild emotions. Cam was Cam; he always had been, he always would be. Being brothers, and twins, Coy probably knew him better than anyone. He knew he had a good heart. He knew he was caring and generous, and he knew he was horrible at expressing those traits. Generally, he gave him a pass and accepted the fact that he wasn't the world's greatest communicator. But if he hurt Ivy with his callous thoughtlessness then Coy would be unable to ignore the situation.

He stood on the porch another minute, trying to make his tired foggy brain work. If he left Cam to himself, he would no doubt mess things up and Ivy would be hurt. In order to keep that from happening, he would have to throw himself under the bus and act as her emotional bodyguard. And in order to do that, he would have to spend lots of time with the two of them running interference. At least that was the reason he gave himself for deciding to spend as much time as possible with Ivy while she was here. Beyond that he wouldn't let himself dwell too closely on his intentions.

The smell of food wafted out onto the porch, reminding him he was famished. He walked into the kitchen and came to a screeching halt at the sight of Ivy wearing a bathrobe and sitting at the kitchen table talking to Cade. Once again he was thankful for Layla. Cade could be incredibly charming when he wanted to be and girls had always liked him, wheelchair or no wheelchair. But since he had met and fallen for Layla, he had no interest in anyone else. Now he and Ivy were chatting like old friends as she drank something warm and ate a sandwich. Almost as if she sensed his presence, she turned toward him with a ready smile.

"Come and eat," she said, jumping up and looking around for something to fix him.

"Sit," he said. "I can get it." He laid his hand on her shoulder and tried to push her back down, but she seemed uncertain of what to do.

"Or you could both sit, and I could fix the food," Cade said dryly. He wheeled himself to the refrigerator and began pulling out sandwich fixings.

Ivy sat, and so did Coy. "Wow, Cade is fixing me food and all it took was a horrific crash and three days in the wilderness," Coy said.

Cade laughed. "Please. If Ivy wasn't here, you know you'd be fixing your own food. I'm trying to make a good impression and show her we have good manners in Montana."

"Oh don't bother, Cade," Ivy said. "I spent three days with Coy. I know better." She patted his hand where it lay on the table and then set it back in her lap with a frown of confusion.

He knew exactly how she felt. After all their intimate contact the past three days, touching each other felt natural. But now they were back where everything was upside down. For instance, she was Cam's girl here, and not Coy's to take care of.

An awkward silence fell over the room while Cade worked on

preparing Coy's food and Coy and Ivy tried to sort out their mixed up emotions. Coy realized Ivy hadn't touched her food.

"Eat," he commanded.

"I tried," she said. "I can only take a few bites at a time. I think my stomach shrunk." She pressed her hand to her abdomen.

"Are you okay?" Coy asked anxiously.

"I'm fine," she said automatically.

"I've heard that somewhere before," he said.

They laughed together. She reached up to touch his head which was still crusted with blood and slightly swollen. "How's the head?" she asked.

He closed his eyes and forced himself not to lean into her touch. "It doesn't hurt anymore."

"Maybe you should have a doctor look at it, in case," she suggested.

"Maybe you could pretend I'm a horse and work your magic diagnosing me."

"I don't think so," she replied. "I don't think you want me to run my hands down your flank."

Not until Cade sputtered a laugh did she realize what she said or how it sounded. "I'm very sleep deprived," she explained, dropping her head into her hands to cover her mortification.

Thankfully Layla came into the room then. "There. Your clothes are in the washer. The good news is I don't think any of them are going to stain."

"What's the bad news?" Cade asked.

"There is no bad news," she replied.

"My little optimist," he said, smiling at her.

"You're cooking for Coy?" she asked as she surveyed the spread of food on the counter.

"Technically, I'm assembling food for Coy."

"I'm still very proud," she said. "Let me show you to your room, Ivy. I set out a bunch of toiletries for you to use until yours get here. Then I thought you might want to take a nap."

Ivy turned to look at Cade. "Marry her," she said.

He laughed. "Don't worry, I plan to." He watched the girls exit the room and turned to Coy. "She seems nice."

"Yeah," Coy said. He, too, was staring after the girls. "She's sweet. And funny. You know she didn't complain once the entire time? I didn't like her at first, but somewhere along the way that changed."

"So I noticed," Cade said.

"What?" Coy said absently.

"You're still staring at empty air with a goofy grin on your face," Cade said. He wheeled himself next to Coy and set the sandwich on the table. "This isn't going to end well for you."

Coy groaned. "Tell me about it." He blew out a breath. "What's up with Cam, anyway? He's barely glanced at her since we got here?"

"Asking what's wrong with Cam is like asking why cows moo. It is what it is. Cam doesn't make sense to you or me because you and I are more like each other than we're like him. Maybe you should ask Josh for some insight."

Coy groaned again at the thought of asking his youngest, most taciturn brother for advice. "I'm not that desperate. Yet. Thanks for the sandwich."

"So tell me all about the journey, MacGyver," Cade said. And in between bites of food, Coy did exactly that.

✳ ✳ ✳

IN THE GUEST room down the hall, Ivy dropped the borrowed bathrobe and stared at herself in the mirror. She was bruised, scratched and dirty from head to foot. Her nails were torn and covered with pine sap.

"No wonder," she muttered. No wonder Cam had practically run away screaming at the sight of her. She would have done the same thing. She only hoped she could put herself back together and somehow look presentable again.

As she stepped into the shower, she shuddered when the hot water hit her skin. It was odd how after only three days of being in the wilderness, she had almost forgotten what modern amenities felt like.

Now, being in the warm glow of electricity with hot running water on her skin, she felt like a visitor to a strange land. Maybe because she actually was a visitor to a strange land.

She hadn't expected Montana to be as different from Kentucky as it was. In Kentucky, she was known by her family's name and her brothers' reputations. Everyone knew she was little Ivy Honeywell, youngest child of the Lexington Honeywells, and the only girl among boys who had become legendary for their wild pranks. But here, she was only Ivy, Cam's girl with the funny accent. Despite how much she had wanted to get away from her brothers and make her own way, she found herself feeling lonely and bereft. And Cam's initial reaction to her hadn't helped much. In fact, it had sort of hurt. In addition to looking at her as if she were something that crawled out from under a rock, he hadn't said one word to her or asked about her wellbeing.

It was difficult, if not impossible, not to contrast that with Coy who hadn't stopped asking if she was all right. Unbidden, her thoughts turned to two nights ago when she had asked Coy if he thought she was pretty.

I think you're about the prettiest thing I've ever seen, he had replied.

Tears blurred her vision and she shoved her head under the spray to wash them away. All in all, Montana was turning out to be a very confusing place. Refusing to allow herself to dwell on her morose thoughts anymore, she concentrated on getting clean.

Layla's bath products smelled heavenly, and felt even better on her skin. She gloried in the lather, sweet scent, and moisture, washing her hair and body twice. When she was finished with her shower, she tried scrubbing her fingernails with a brush to remove the pine sap, but it wouldn't budge. When her toiletries arrived, she would use nail polish remover to try and dissolve the sap. And she would give herself a manicure. In fact, she would make herself look so good Cam wouldn't be able to resist her.

With that thought in mind, she put on Layla's nightgown, crawled between the sheets and closed her eyes. She tried to summon a picture of Cam's face to lull her to sleep, but no matter how hard she tried, Coy's dimple and curly hair refused to go away. Her hand reached to the space beside her, grasping at nothing. She almost expected him to be beside her and was surprised at how empty she felt without him.

She frowned at the ceiling. She had slept alone for twenty two years. Why after three nights sleeping next to Coy did the space feel lonely? After failing to find a solution to that puzzling question, she gave up trying. Instead, she propped a pillow behind her back, hugged another to her chest, then cuddled into the fetal position and fell asleep.

CHAPTER 11

*I*vy slept a long time. Coy showered and walked to the office to check on Cam's progress. As he had suspected, Cam had already sent a truck to pick up Tanner, called a tow for their wrecked truck, talked to an insurance adjuster, and moved on to regular ranch business.

"Are our insurance rates going to go up?" Coy asked, sitting down across from his brother.

"A little," Cam said, not taking his eyes from the computer.

By his subdued expression, Coy knew he was no longer worried about the money. That was Cam's way; he acted like a boor until he became accustomed to a new situation, and then he accepted it with no further complaint.

"Ivy's nice. I like her," Coy said, an understatement if he had ever said one.

"Told you that you would if you took the time to get to know her," Cam said in the same subdued tone.

"Are you guys serious?" Coy asked.

Cam grunted in response.

"What does that mean?"

Cam finally removed his eyes from the computer. "It means I don't know."

Coy's heart began to beat hard with hopeful anticipation. "You don't know? How could you not know? You invited her here."

"I invited her here to try and figure out if there's anything between us. She's nice, as you said. And she's from a good family."

"What does her family have to do with it?" Coy asked.

"Everything. You wouldn't want a girl from a bad family," Cam said.

"But Layla doesn't have any family, and we love her."

Cam paused. "That's true. But Layla's the exception. A good family is an important qualification for a future wife."

"Wife," Coy gasped. "You're not thinking of marrying her."

"Why not?" Cam shrugged. "We're old enough. Cade's already practically engaged, and he's two years younger. It would be nice to have this part of my life taken care of."

Coy was genuinely disturbed by his brother's businesslike tone. "You make it sound like she's here to interview for a job."

"In some ways I suppose she is," Cam said. "Don't give me that look. I know how it sounds, but I have to be practical. Montana isn't for everyone. The ranch is remote. Some women don't want to live their lives surrounded by cowboys and animals with no malls or movie theaters nearby. Winters are harsh. Life isn't easy here, and before I marry a woman I want to know she can hack it."

"Believe me when I tell you Ivy can," Coy said tersely. "But what about love?"

"If you set the stage correctly, love will follow."

"You're talking about an arranged marriage," Coy said, his lip curling in disgust.

"No I'm not. I'm talking about being cautious. And, as an added bonus to marrying Ivy, I could expand our business into the horse sector. She's good at what she does, and the Honeywell name carries, even out here. Did you know last year her family had four horses in the derby? They're the big time in the horse world. I've been crunching some numbers, and with her help we could double our assets in a few years."

Coy stared at his brother as if he had never seen him before, and maybe he hadn't. Was he as cold as he sounded? If so, how had he gotten that way? Not from their upbringing, that was for certain. Their parents were warm and loving people. He stood, trying hard to control his temper.

"If you want to run your personal life like a business, then that's your prerogative. But don't apply your tactics to Ivy. She came here because she likes you and if she learns you're using her to further the ranch, I will personally drive her back to Kentucky after putting my fist in your face." With that he slammed out of the office, leaving Cam staring after him in mute shock.

What had gotten into Coy? Cam had never seen him angry before. Maybe it was the ordeal he had been through. He had to be exhausted, and his head still sported an angry-looking bruise. Giving up trying to figure out his brother, he returned his attention to the numbers on the screen. Coy was Coy. Who knew what went on in his head? From their earliest experiences, Coy had had no head for business. He had always been a people person. As a team, they worked well together. Cam made the difficult decisions, and Coy softened the delivery. Cam didn't begrudge the fact that people liked his twin better. In every business, someone had to be the number cruncher. Someone had to be the one who cut expenses and salaries. In their operation, that was Cam.

At first when they took over the business for their father, things had been hard for Cam. He felt things much deeper than anyone guessed. Then he realized he had the capacity to compartmentalize difficult things. He wasn't sure when he started compartmentalizing everything, cutting off all emotion so he went through his days feeling nothing. But since that time, life had been much easier for him. Maybe people thought he was heartless, and maybe he was. But he had a job to do, and there was no one else to do it.

Without another thought for anything but the numbers on the screen, he adjusted his chair and went back to work.

* * *

COY STALKED TO THE HOUSE, but by the time he reached the living room, his anger had been replaced by exhaustion. He sat in the recliner and glanced down the hall toward Ivy's room, wondering if she was okay. Should he check on her? The temptation to walk down the hall, curl up beside her, and nap was almost overwhelming. But of course no one would understand the bond their adventure had forged between them. Besides being a really bad idea, sleeping beside her would cause a scandal the size of Montana. And yet, despite the impossibility of such a suggestion, it was exactly what he yearned to do.

He supposed with time, the feeling would fade. No doubt their fear and insecurity had created an unnatural dependence on each other. But because he understood why he was feeling such a desperate need to go to her didn't stop him from feeling bereft without her. Eventually, he drifted off to sleep.

He woke to a cool hand gently touching his forehead and he smiled before opening his eyes. *Ivy.*

"Coy, are you doing okay? Can I bring you anything?"

His eyes opened and blinked a couple of times. "Layla," he said questioningly.

"Are you feeling up to supper? It's ready," she said gently.

He swallowed hard, trying to clear away the lingering vision of Ivy. "I'm fine," he said automatically. He shifted his chair into a sitting position. "Is Ivy awake?"

Layla smiled. "Come and see for yourself." She turned and led the way into the kitchen with Coy trailing intently behind her. But when he entered the kitchen he stopped short and stared. He almost didn't recognize the woman in front of him. Once again she looked like the ice princess he had first seen. She was dressed in light gray trousers, perfectly tailored to fit her. Her top was a soft pink color. She was perfectly made up with perfectly coiffed hair. Even her nails looked perfect. And beside her sat Cam, beaming with approval and leaning toward her like she was his every dream come true.

Coy was prepared for the raw fist of jealousy the image caused him. He swallowed it down by concentrating on the food. He was still famished. Layla had probably guessed as much because, if the full table was any indication, she had prepared extra. He filled his plate and sat beside Cade. The meal was already in progress, so he began eating without hesitation, unabashedly eavesdropping on the conversation between Cam and Ivy.

Unsurprisingly, they were talking horses. She sounded as remote as she looked. This wasn't the same passionate creature he had spent the last three days with. Instead, she sounded like a true business professional as she relayed breeding practices and lineages from her ranch. He actually felt somewhat cheered as he listened to her talk. Maybe she was the ice princess he had first presumed. Maybe their time in the wilderness had been a fluke. Maybe she was the girl who wore well-tailored expensive business suits, and not the girl who wore jeans and a well-worn hoodie. Maybe she was better suited for Cam, after all.

"Oh, by the way, I called your family while you were sleeping," Cam told her.

She froze, her fork halfway to her mouth. "You called my family." She said the words slowly, set down her fork, and placed her hand in her lap.

"Yes," Cam said. He was aware he had upset her, but he had no idea how. "I tried to call them when you went missing, but no one was home."

"They were visiting some friends," she said.

"Right. So I figured I would give them a heads up in case word somehow got back to them. I didn't want them to worry. I told them you had been lost, but you were fine and would call them when you woke up." Cam spoke with the conviction of someone who knew he had done the right thing, the sensible thing. He had even been a little proud of his thoughtfulness in remembering her family, knowing they would be panicked if they somehow heard the news she had been lost.

Ivy swallowed hard before speaking again. "Who exactly did you talk to?"

Cam waved his hand in the air. "One of your brothers. I don't know which one."

The color drained from Ivy's face. She turned stricken eyes to Coy who was giving her a sympathetic smile. "Can I use your phone, please?" she whispered to the room at large.

"Sure," Layla replied for all of them. "Use the one in the den so you won't be disturbed."

"Thank you." Ivy barely managed to get the words past her numb lips. She pushed away from the table and stumbled down the hall toward the den. Her fingers were shaking so badly it took her four tries before she could dial the number correctly.

"Hello."

She winced when she heard her brother's voice. It was Brent, the oldest. "Brent, it's me, Ivy."

There was a significant pause before he spoke again. "Well, well, the prodigal daughter."

It would be more prudent to ignore that. "I'm calling to let y'all know I'm fine. Really. There's no need for you to come here."

"We'll see," he said cryptically, and then he hung up.

She had no idea how long she stood clutching the phone. Eventually Coy was there, gently tugging the phone from her lifeless grasp.

"How did it go?" he asked softly.

"Not well," she replied. She took a shaky breath and tried not to cry as she let it out. He rested his hands on her shoulders, his thumbs making soothing circles.

"What's the worst that could happen?"

"They could come here," she rasped.

"What's so bad about that?"

"You haven't met them."

"I sort of want to," he said, his hands clutching tighter on his shoulders.

She remembered what he had said a couple of days ago about wanting to spend a few minutes alone with each of her brothers. She smiled and relaxed slightly.

"If they come here, we'll deal with it. It will be okay," he said reassuringly.

"It will be okay," she repeated, trying desperately to believe the words.

They looked at each other for a few minutes. At some point, she had put her hands on his chest, clutching his shirt.

"You want some chocolate?" he whispered.

"More than almost anything in the world," she returned.

For the sake of his sanity, he refrained from asking what else she might want more than chocolate at that moment.

CHAPTER 12

That evening was an exercise in frustration for Coy. After supper, Ivy insisted on helping Layla with the dishes. He, Cade and Josh retired to the den while Cam went back to his office to work.

Coy stood looking out the den window. "Do you think he'll stay out there all night?"

"With Cam, it's hard to say," Cade said.

"He'll be back," Josh volunteered. "He doesn't want to hang around and do nothing while he's waiting on the women to finish cleaning up."

"Can't say I blame him," Cade said, sounding bored. "What did I do with my time before Layla came along?"

"Devised ways to meet girls," Josh said with uncharacteristic good humor.

"You could take a few lessons," Cade said.

"Not me. I only plan to date one girl, ever. I don't like the idea of dating a lot of different girls."

"Sometimes you have to sift through a lot of rocks before you find the piece of gold," Coy answered absently.

"I know you're in trouble if you've turned philosophical," Cade said.

"What are you talking about?" Josh asked.

"Nothing," Coy and Cade answered together. Josh would never understand the ethical dilemma of one brother wanting another brother's girl. His world was still black and white. Maybe it always would be; he was that type of kid.

The girls' happy chatter and laughter filtered down the hall, causing the brothers to smile, even Josh.

"It's nice to have girls in the house," he said.

"Maybe all hope for you isn't lost," Cade muttered under his breath.

Coy didn't comment, but he agreed with Josh. The female presence added something special to the house, making it feel more like a home than a house. The girls finished with the kitchen and came down the hall to the den. Cade's face lit like a Roman candle when he saw Layla. Coy wondered if he looked at Ivy the same way. He felt like he did, like a switch had been flipped and all was right with the world again. Instinctively, they took a step toward each other, then stopped, trying to figure out what to do next.

"I heard there are new kittens in the barn," Cade said to Layla. "Want to go check?"

"You know I'm a sucker for kittens," she said. "Want to come with us, Josh?"

Josh couldn't hide his surprise at the invitation. Layla and Cade were well known for seeking some privacy in the evenings, away from the rest of the family. But he didn't turn down the invitation. The room felt tense, and he had no idea why. Getting outside would be a relief.

"Sure," he said. He turned back to Coy and Ivy. "Aren't you guys coming?"

"Maybe later," Coy answered for both of them.

Josh nodded and hurried off to follow Layla and Cade down the hallway.

"You didn't want to go with them, did you?" Coy asked Ivy.

She shook her head. She looked as cool and pristine as she had when he first saw her. He wished she would change clothes or take her hair down or otherwise give him some signal she was the girl he knew. As if she read his mind, she popped her heels off her feet and gave a sigh of relief before plopping down on the couch and tucking her feet under her.

"I've been dying to do that for hours," she said.

He sat beside her. "Why do you wear them if they hurt your feet?"

"Because they're pretty," she said, as if the answer should have been obvious.

"Do you really like dressing up like this?" he indicated her outfit with a wave of his hand.

She looked down at herself. "Yes. You have to understand I spent my childhood in castoff team shirts, baseball caps, and sneakers. Everyone thought I was such a tomboy. But the truth was I didn't know anything different. Until I got to high school, and especially to college, I didn't know much about girl stuff. My roommates took me under their collective wing and taught me about clothes, hair and makeup. It was like a whole new, fascinating world. I don't want to look like a man. I want to look and smell like a girl."

Grudgingly, he had to admit that made sense. And there was no arguing with the fact that she looked beautiful this way, with her perfect hair and makeup. But there was something inside him that couldn't let go of the image of her in jeans and a sweatshirt. When she looked that way, he thought of her as his.

"But you do let your hair down sometimes. I mean, you brought casual wear."

"I work out," she told him. "And sometimes I want to relax. Or play ball. But for the most part I try to cultivate a mature and professional image. It's my hope people will someday see me as something other than the youngest Honeywell."

"You've come to the right place," he said. "Here you're just Ivy." *Beautiful, perfect, unobtainable Ivy.*

"That's true."

He searched her face, not understanding the reticence in her tone. "What?"

"I was thinking about this earlier. It's sort of like that old proverb about getting what you wish for. I've always wanted to be away from my family name and influence, but now that I'm here it feels sort of scary."

"You're doing great," he said, smiling sweetly.

There it was again, that unexpected praise. She wasn't sure how, with a few simple words, he had the ability to make her believe everything would be okay. If he thought she would survive if her brothers came to check on her, then she would survive. If he said she was doing great, then she believed she was doing great. If he said she was pretty, she actually felt pretty. Even covered in layers of dirt, he had made her feel beautiful.

"How was your nap?" he asked.

Her brow puckered at the small amount of strain in his tone. Had he guessed she had trouble sleeping without him? That would certainly be mortifying. Unless he had somehow felt the same way.

"It was…okay," she said. "How was yours?"

"Okay," he said softly, his gaze falling to her lips and lingering.

"There you are," Cam said, poking his head around the door. "It's a nice night for a walk. Are you up for it?"

"Sure," Ivy said, hoping her voice didn't sound as shaky as it felt. "Let me put my shoes on." After stuffing her feet into her uncomfortable heels, she said goodbye to Coy without looking at him. She was afraid the sight of him might increase the strange physical ache she felt for him. It would be awkward if she suddenly ran back and clung to him the way she longed to do. Was she losing her mind?

What other explanation could there be for her suddenly tumultuous emotions? Did getting lost in the wilderness often cause these sorts of adverse effects? She came here to visit Cam. She hadn't even liked Coy when she met him. And now she couldn't stop thinking about him. Even as she was walking with Cam, her mind was focused on Coy, wondering if he was okay, wondering if he missed her as much as she missed him.

"Do you think Coy's okay?" she blurted. "I mean, you know him better than I do. He hit his head pretty hard on the truck window. Maybe he should see a doctor, in case."

"He has been acting strangely since he got back," Cam mused, staring off into the distance.

Her heart picked up its pace. Was it because of her? Was Coy dealing with his own confusion over their situation?

"Maybe he's having girl trouble," Cam said. "That's usually what it is with him."

"He dates a lot?" she asked, trying to keep her voice casual.

"All the time," Cam said. "He's never without a girl. He went out with some girl from town the night before he picked you up. He said the date went really well. I guess maybe he's thinking about her. Or any number of other girls. He's never been what you'd call a one-woman kind of guy."

"Hmm." Her tone remained even while inside her heart was plummeting. She remembered the girls who had been working the drive thru of the fast food restaurant. They had fallen all over themselves for Coy as soon as he turned on the charm. Once again, her previous dislike for him rose to the surface. She could never be with someone who blatantly flirted with other girls. A quick glance at Cam told her he wasn't that sort of guy. He wasn't even flirting with *her*, and she was his girlfriend. Sort of.

"Cam," she said tentatively.

"Yes?"

She cleared her throat. Now that she was starting on this path, she wasn't sure how to proceed. "What are we, exactly? I've been trying to find a definition for us, but so far I haven't had any luck. Have you?" She stopped and leaned against a fencepost.

Cam stopped too, staring at her. She looked incredibly pretty at this moment. She made it easy to forget his first sight of her. Of course he knew she had spent three days in the wilderness, but somehow he had expected her to look as perfect as she always did when they talked on the internet. Maybe he had built her up in his head to mythological proportions, but the Ivy he knew was cool and composed. She could handle anything, do anything. And she would have come out of the wilderness as perfect as she went in. In his head, he knew he was being unreasonable, but his heart couldn't accept any disillusionment in the woman he had created. Ivy was perfect, and she was his.

"We're...seeing where things go, I suppose." He looked at her uncertainly. "Is that a bad answer? I've never been very good at saying the right thing at the right time. I usually have the opposite problem."

She smiled. "No, I think that's a great answer."

This was the part where he was supposed to make some move toward her. Standing as she was, leaning against the fencepost and illuminated by the soft lamplight behind her, it was the perfect moment for a kiss. But somehow he couldn't bring himself to kiss her. Coy would have kissed her. Cade would have kissed her. Josh, well, Josh would have run away screaming. But regardless of what he knew he should do, he couldn't. And then the moment was gone. Swallowing convulsively, she looked away from him and he knew she felt the sting of his rejection.

Guilt heaped on top of his other swirling emotions, adding to the mix and muddying the waters.

"I heard there are some new kittens in the barn," she whispered at last. "Want to come look with me?"

He was allergic to cats, but he couldn't reject her twice in one evening. "Sure," he said. "It's probably that barn." He pointed to their horse barn and followed behind her as she led the way.

CHAPTER 13

There was movement in the kitchen and the yard, but Ivy ignored it, choosing instead to remain in bed. It was barely past dawn and she had a little leeway before she would be considered rude for sleeping in. Although, sleeping had little part in why she was still in bed. Once again she had slept fitfully, tossing and turning and waking every few minutes to turn beside her, looking for Coy.

What was she doing here? Maybe she should cut her losses and go back to Kentucky now. But even as she thought it, she rejected the idea. Here she was in emotional turmoil. At home, she would be at the mercy of her brothers' teasing. They were already angry she went away without informing them. She could only imagine what they would say if she returned before her time was up. And even if they miraculously refrained from teasing her, they might feel she had returned home because she sensed their disapproval. No, going home early wasn't an option.

So what was she to do? She had come here for Cam. In person, he was everything he seemed to be long distance: reserved, in charge, and structured. He would never tease her. He would never flirt with other girls. He would be a good provider. In a word, he was safe. But now that she was here, she wasn't sure she wanted him. Even worse, she was pretty certain he didn't want her. His disappointment and rejection were intensely painful. She had spent the past year building him up in her head. On paper, he was perfect for her. He was supposed to be her knight in shining armor. Instead, his attention to her was passive at best and nonexistent at worst.

And then there was Coy. He came out of nowhere, turning from an enemy to a friend to...what? What were they to each other? Their three days together in the wilderness had been a step out of time, a blip. The forced time together was something that rarely happened to people and therefore she had nothing to compare it to. Would her connection to him fade in time? Was he constantly on her mind because, for a time, he had been her only source of security and comfort? Or was there something deeper between them?

With a sigh, she discounted that idea. Hadn't Cam confirmed her suspicions about Coy? He was a playboy, as she first thought. Either her feelings weren't mutual, or he was playing with her. He couldn't be as confused as she was; no one in history had been as confused as she was.

The minutes ticked as she stared at the ceiling, trying and failing to find a solution to her dilemma. At last, she decided she wouldn't find any answers written on the drywall. For today, she would have to take events as they happened. Cam had asked her to look at the horses with him and she focused on getting ready.

Cade and Layla were the only ones in the kitchen when she emerged from her bedroom. She wondered why they both paused and looked at her in astonishment before continuing with their conversation.

"I'm spending the day looking over the horses with Cam," she announced.

"Sounds like a plan," Cade said. "And what are you going to do today, Miss?" He turned loving eyes to Layla.

"I'm going to finish the laundry and then I'm going to make lasagna for supper."

"Lasagna is my favorite food," he said.

"It is?" she asked with mock innocence. "I had no idea." She made the mistake of walking too close to him. He caught her around the waist and pulled her close. She framed his face with her hands and they shared a smile that spoke of love, intimacy, and understanding. Ivy felt like an intruder, and an envious one at that. Their obvious devotion to each other made her situation all the more painful.

"Hey," Coy spoke softly from the doorway, startling her from her trance. When she turned to face him, he looked her up and down with one eyebrow raised.

"I'm seeing the horses today with Cam," she told him.

"Yes I see."

She looked down at her English riding habit. "I guess no one dresses this formally here, huh?"

"No, but that doesn't mean you can't. You're bringing sophistication to the wilds of Montana. I'm only sorry we don't have an English saddle for you."

"S'okay," she said, causing him to smile. They had no idea they were staring at each other until Cade cleared his throat.

"Cam's probably waiting. You know how he is about his schedule," he said.

"Right," Coy said. "Ready?"

She blinked at him. "You're coming with us?"

"Wouldn't miss it," Coy said. "I want to see you work your magic with the horses again. Why? Don't you want me along?"

"No, I, I mean, yes, I mean…" She turned to look helplessly at Cade and Layla who were watching her and Coy like they were a soap opera on television.

"You'll have a great day," Layla said reassuringly. Ivy smiled at her. She really did think she had found a kindred spirit in Layla. Already she would be sad when she had to leave her.

"See you guys later," she said, giving them a small wave.

"This is a good day to look at the horses," Coy told her. "One of our mares foaled in the night." They walked side by side, their arms swinging between them. He itched to reach over and clasp her hand. He wondered if she felt the same way because she moved her hands to clasp nervously in front of her, making her stride awkward.

"I was about to send someone to check on you," Cam said when he met them at the door of the barn. He did clasp Ivy's hand and led her to a wide pen strewn with new hay. "I want you to take a look at this fella, Ivy. He was born a few hours ago. He's beautiful, but he's not acting right." He stood aside so she could see the new little foal for herself.

Ivy took a look at the snow white foal and sucked in a breath. Cam hadn't been exaggerating; the horse was beautiful. His whiteness was marred only by one small black spot near his tail. Her heart sank as she looked at his mother, a beautiful frame pinto. Without hesitation, she climbed the fence and entered the pen.

"Have you had this mare long?" she asked.

"No, we just bought her. I paid a little extra because she was already pregnant."

"You should probably get some of your money back," Ivy said sadly. She knelt beside the little foal and looked in its eyes. "This foal will be dead by nightfall."

"What?" Cam asked, leaning forward over the fence in alarm. "Why?"

"OLWS," she said.

Coy sucked in a breath. He had heard of the genetic defect, but had never seen it in person. It was a horrible disease, producing beautiful white foals like this one. They usually died within a matter of hours because their intestines weren't hooked to the outsides of their bodies. Initially, they ate and played like other foals, but as time went on, they started to exhibit signs of distress until they ultimately dropped dead or were euthanized.

"Are you sure?" Cam asked.

Ivy nodded. "You can tell by the eyes. See how they're a grayish color? If you have a trustworthy vet, I would get a second opinion, but you should probably tell him to bring supplies to put this one down." She gave the foal a gentle pat and watched him with sad eyes before her expression turned hard. "Have you used this breeder often?"

"No, only a few times."

"OLWS is irresponsible. A simple genetics test would prevent it from happening. We test all our mares and studs for a range of problems. Any reliable breeder should do the same." Frame horses, those with white splotches, were often at risk of carrying the genetic quirk that caused OLWS. Because frame horses were prized for their beauty, it was common to breed two frame horses together. But without genetic testing to determine if two carriers were being bred together, such practices were like playing Russian roulette. The same pair of horses could breed multiple times with no problems before producing an OLWS foal. A breeder who didn't take proper precaution by not breeding two OLWS carriers together cared more about the bottom line than the quality and comfort of his animals, in Ivy's opinion.

"I can't say I disagree with you," Cam said.

Ivy stood, dusted herself off, and mounted the fence. Coy waited for Cam to step forward and lift her down, but Cam remained deep in thought, staring at the doomed foal.

Coy put his hands up and easily lifted her down, thinking as he did so of the night she fell asleep in his arms. He had carried her to the shelter, tucked her under the blankets, then fell asleep beside her. His heart pinged as their eyes made contact and lingered. Was she remembering the same thing?

"Thank you," she said softly, giving his chest a gentle pat. He dropped his hands and stepped back as Cam stepped forward.

"Ready?" Cam asked. His tone was disheartened, but Coy knew it was because he had learned his new, expensive foal was a goner.

"Ready," Ivy said. Cam led them through the barn, stopping at each horse and explaining its parentage while Ivy's hands roamed over the animal with expertise, searching for he knew not what. Like most ranchers, he had a basic understanding of horses, but his main focus was cattle because they were their bread and butter. It was interesting to see this side of Ivy—the professional who had generations of experience in her genes.

While Cam talked, Ivy remained silent, suspiciously so. Coy watched her expressions and knew there was a lot she wasn't saying. Finally, they finished their tour of the horse barn.

"Well, what's the verdict?" Cam asked.

Ivy bit her lip, looking uncertainly between the two brothers. "How honest do you want me to be?"

"Brutally," Cam said.

"Your breeder is almost criminally irresponsible. Five of your horses show signs of osteochondrosis, three of them also have epiphysitis. In my opinion, their growth was rushed with cheap fillers when they were foals. The breeder tried to cut corners and your horses are suffering. I can't say for sure, but I'm concerned some of them are showing the beginnings of arthritis."

Cam blew out a breath. Their horses were part of their livelihood. They couldn't afford to lose them. "Is there anything we can do?"

"I'll review their feed. There are certain minerals that might help; I'll need to make sure they're getting those. There are some therapies I can recommend, and of course they'll need to rotate duty whenever possible. But my best advice is to find another breeder as soon as possible."

"I'm working on it," Cam said, throwing her a significant look.

She wasn't sure what to say to that. Neither was Coy, apparently, if the choking noise he made was any indication. He coughed and turned away to cover his mouth with his elbow.

Now, of all times Cam decided to turn into Casanova? At least Coy could be thankful Ivy's reaction had been as shocked as his. And Cam seemed oblivious to them both. Still, the proclamation had hit him like a sledgehammer. And that was when Coy came to a startling realization. If things worked out between Cam and Ivy, there was no way he could stand by and happily watch them together day in and day out on the ranch. He would have to go away, as far away as possible. He smiled wryly. Maybe if she came here, he could go to Kentucky and fill her spot. True, he wouldn't know as much about horses as she did, but he was good with animals and a hard worker. And Kentucky was far enough away that maybe he would be able to get the space he would need to heal.

Ivy was recovering from her shock when she saw Coy's amused smile. Had she mistaken the choking sound for laughter? Was he really entertained by the idea of her marrying Cam and becoming their new breeder?

"Ivy, do you need to eat something? You're looking a little pale," Coy said.

"I, yes, maybe. What time is it?"

Cam checked his watch. "It's noon. Why don't you guys go on? I have some calls to make. I'll meet up with you later." He turned and walked away, leaving Ivy frowning after him.

"What he meant to say was thanks for looking at the horses this morning. Gee, it's swell to have you here," Coy said.

Ivy laughed. They turned toward the house and fell in step together. "I suppose it's not easy to be the one in charge," she said.

"No, it's not. And I'm guilty of helping to make Cam the way he is. I like working with the animals and the people, but not papers and computers. Someone had to do it. Cam stepped up."

Coy was being very generous, she thought, in taking responsibility for his brother's faults. She slipped her hand into the crook of his arm. "You're a nice person, Coy."

"I'm glad you think so," he said. "I know I didn't make a good first impression."

"I think both of us should make a rule not to trust our first impressions from now on," she said.

He smiled. "The strangers at the drive thru liked me better than you did."

She frowned, thinking of the drive thru workers and their over the top reactions to his flirtation. "You said you didn't have a girlfriend," she reminded him.

"I don't," he replied indignantly, confused by her accusatory tone.

"Cam said you had a date the night before you met me at the airport."

"Oh. That."

"He said you've had a lot of dates with a lot of girls," she added.

They stopped and faced each other in the doorway of the house. "I have, but nothing serious."

"You must enjoy the thrill of the hunt," she said.

He weighed his words carefully before he spoke. "I suppose every man enjoys the chase. But mostly what kept me going was the hope I might someday find what I was looking for."

The unconscious part of her brain acknowledged he spoke in the past tense. "And what are you looking for?" she asked.

Before he could answer, Josh tripped up the porch steps. He tipped his hat to them, said, "Excuse me," and then squeezed by Coy, causing him to step forward toward Ivy. He grasped her elbows to avoid smashing her into the doorframe.

"I'll know it when I see it," he said, his thumbs smoothing over the points of her elbows. "Are you ready?"

"For what?" she whispered.

He grinned at her. "Lunch."

CHAPTER 14

Cam showed up as everyone else was finishing lunch.

"Sorry about that," he said. "I was making some calls about the breeder we discussed. Turns out a couple of other ranchers have had OLWS foals, too." He sat and nodded appreciatively at Layla when she set food in front of him.

"That really boils my blood," Ivy said, causing everyone at the table to smile at her unique turn of phrase.

"Mine too," Cam said, although neither his expression nor tone changed. "Want to tour some more of the ranch with me after lunch?"

"Okay," she said, feeling suddenly shy. At least she hoped what she was feeling was shyness. This was what she came here for, why did she feel reluctant?

"Are you sure you're going to be able to ride western?" Coy teased. "You might fall off with all that room to roam around."

"I could ride bareback if I had to," she said smugly.

Cade whistled. "That shut you up," he said to Coy.

"There's no need for anyone to ride bareback," Cam said mildly. "I had an English saddle made for Ivy."

Everyone stopped talking to stare at him.

"That was very sweet, Cam. Thank you," Ivy said. She was humbled by the magnitude of the gift. Custom-made saddles weren't cheap. Being an accomplished rider, she could have used the bulkier western saddle with no problem, although she did prefer the lighter, straighter English saddles she used at home. For Cam to have had an expensive saddle made for her spoke volumes, not only about his intentions, but also about his thoughtfulness and attention to detail. "Let me freshen up and I'll be ready to go." She escaped to her bedroom, not looking at Coy as she exited the kitchen. Once she was out of sight of the kitchen, she flew down the hall to her room, opened the door, then closed it and leaned against it.

There was a small part of her that wanted Cam to be the bad guy in this scenario. She wanted to take his indifference and lack of attention and hold it against him, making Coy the clear cut winner in their messed up triangle. But that wasn't fair. She knew the way Cam was when she agreed to come here. In the twelve months they had been communicating, he had never misrepresented himself to her. He hadn't tried to pretend he was overly passionate or attentive. He had presented himself as a rock-steady, nice guy, and that was what he was turning out to be. It was what she had wanted up until a few days ago when she became stranded with Coy.

Now his sweet, sunny personality and easy affection were ruining everything.

Pull yourself together, she commanded. She took a few deep breaths, opened the door, and went back to the kitchen. By the time she reached the door, she was able to summon a smile. "Ready."

Cam stood and they walked out of the kitchen together.

Josh stood after they left the room. "Tanner and I are repairing some fencing in the north pasture. I'll probably be late for supper."

"Here, take a snack and something to drink," Layla said. She reached into the fridge and handed him a brown paper bag of prepared snacks she kept on hand for the times then they would be working through meals.

After Josh left, she sat down at the table beside Cade. He rested his arm on the back of her chair and began absently playing with her hair.

"So Cam has game. Who knew?" Cade said.

Coy rested his elbows on the table and hung his head between his hands. "He bought her a saddle. Wow. How am I supposed to compete with that?"

"Coy, the way to a girl's heart isn't through leather," Layla pointed out.

"Do you *want* to compete with him?" Cade asked.

"No. Yes. No. I don't know." He rested his head on his arms. "This is horrible. You guys make it look too easy."

"You're obviously forgetting my panicked road trip to Chicago to win her back," Cade said. He and Layla shared a gooey smile.

"Oh, right. I had forgotten that." He blew out a breath. "Maybe this would be easier if I could get a read on Cam. He barely looked twice at her when we finally made it here. He made romance sound like a business decision. And now all of a sudden…" He trailed off.

"But it's not all of a sudden," Layla said gently. "You're forgetting they've been talking for the past year. They have a relationship."

"But she and I have a relationship, too," Coy protested.

"And you and he are twins. Don't forget," Cade added seriously. "Are you going to let her come between you?"

"I don't know," Coy said miserably. "I don't know anything anymore."

"You need to blow off some steam. Go work on the fence with Josh and Tanner," Cade suggested.

"You're right. I need to get out of here. Thanks." He stood and practically fled from the kitchen.

Cade and Layla looked at each other. "I'm worried about him, about both of them," she said. "And Ivy. I don't want anyone to get hurt."

"Someone is going to," Cade predicted. "There's no way for this to end with everyone happy."

"I was so happy for Cam when he told me he was bringing her here. I thought maybe he had finally found true love. But when I see the way Coy looks at her…"

"Is it the way I look at you?" Cade interrupted.

"It is," she said seriously. "But he's right about Cam. He's too good at hiding his emotions. I can't get a read on him." Her brow puckered as she stared at the blank wall across from her.

Cade leaned forward, cinching his arm around her and drawing her to his side. "Want to hear some good news?"

She nodded.

"We're never going to have to go through any of that uncertainty again."

She beamed at him and slipped her arms around his neck. "That's the best news I've heard in a long time," she said, then she tipped her face up to receive his kiss.

* * *

IVY WAS NOT HAVING a good time, and she felt bad about that. Now in the back of her mind there was always the question of whether or not things would be different if she and Coy hadn't spent their time in the woods. Would she have tried harder to make conversation with Cam as they rode around the ranch? Would the silence have felt comfortable instead of awkward? Would she be thinking about Cam and hoping he would kiss her instead of wondering where Coy was and what he was doing? And always in the back of her mind was that niggling feeling of guilt that told her she was being disloyal for thinking of one brother when she was with the other.

The ranch was undeniably beautiful, however, and worked to take some of the focus off her inner turmoil. While her home in Kentucky was lush and rolling, the terrain here was sparser and rockier while still dotted with the occasional verdant, flat pasture or wildflower-strewn meadow. In the distance she could make out a mountain, its top covered with snow. She shivered, thinking how glad she was she and Coy hadn't been stranded up there. No doubt they wouldn't have survived the elements.

The snow that had so impeded their progress home was now gone thanks to the moderate daylight temperatures. At night, the thermometer still dipped below freezing, but now that she was safe and warm at the ranch, she had no reason to resent the cold weather.

"Maybe we'll have a fire tonight," Cam said, making her wonder if he was also thinking about the weather. How sad if that were the case. For the last twelve months they hadn't run out of conversation. Although, looking back, she tried to think if they ever talked about their personal lives. Most of their amusing anecdotes had revolved around their animals. While revealing the facts of their lives to each other, they hadn't revealed many emotions. At the time, she had appreciated his reserve. She would have felt foolish to pour out her heart over a web chat, and she would have felt wary of Cam if he had done the same.

But would she have been so reserved with Coy? Coy, with his sunny, say-what- you're-feeling personality would no doubt have made her laugh with stories of what was happening at the ranch. He would have felt no compunctions over ending each call by telling her he missed her and wanted to be with her. Cam's usual "take care" had felt warm at the time and now, in comparison, felt cold and impersonal.

Then she came back to the same argument she'd had from the beginning: she wasn't supposed to compare them. They were as different as night and day, and it was wrong to pit them against each other. She had never been one of those girls who thrived on drama. Since her brothers created all the drama she could handle, she simply wanted a nice, quiet life for herself. How, then, did she find herself caught between two brothers? And twins, no less. Was there some secret part of her that had craved intrigue all along?

She didn't have much experience with dating, so it was hard to say. The few men she had been able to sneak under her brothers' radar had been casual and occasional dates, nothing serious. Few men were willing to take on five older brothers who scared the living daylights out of most people they came in contact with.

She paused in her reflections to frown. How was it possible out of her five siblings none of them was an introvert? Every single one of them was boisterous and outgoing. They were all carbon copies of each other, practically interchangeable. Even she, who had grown up with them and knew them as well as anybody, had trouble pointing out distinct differences in their personalities. They even looked alike. Their matching dark hair and dark eyes had been one more weapon to use against her. With her blond hair and blue eyes that matched no one else in the family, they had easily convinced her she was adopted.

Not until she was a teenager and demanded a DNA test from her mother did her parents realize how deeply she had taken her brothers' teasing over her parentage. Her mother, instead of getting the requested test, had instead forced her brothers to do a detailed family history, complete with pictures, to show Ivy where her blond hair and blue eyes came from. She had also forced them each to write a short story for Ivy detailing how they had been present for her birth and held her a short while after she exited their mother's womb.

Ivy smiled. That had been a glorious day, when her brothers finally got some comeuppance. What they needed was a little more of that in their lives. On and on her thoughts swirled, thinking of anything but the man beside her who seemed content to keep silent and ride. Eventually, she realized they had turned and were headed back to the ranch. She wondered if Cam became cognizant of the silence between them because he began to point out different features on the ranch. She listened interestedly, enjoying the tour.

By the time they arrived back at the ranch, they were talking and laughing together like the friends they had become over the last year. She was still laughing at a story he told her about one of his ancestors when she looked in the yard and saw something that made her laughter turn into a cry of alarm. Up ahead, Coy was dismounting his own horse, and he was covered in blood.

CHAPTER 15

Coy entered the yard, kicking himself for his own stupidity and carelessness. When he arrived in the pasture to help with the fencing and saw Josh and Tanner turn to him in question, he felt like an idiot. Two people were the ideal number to fix a fence. Three people were extraneous. Deciding he would rather work on a section by himself instead of stand around and feel useless, he moved down the line to another break.

And then, because he was distracted and feeling morose, he became careless, which was never a good thing to be when working with razor-sharp barbed wire. With the claw of his hammer, he caught the wire and pulled taut, then reached behind him to get his stapler, not thinking about the fact that the twisting motion would work to dislodge the wire from his hammer. Because he had been pulling it taut, it sprang back, catching him across the chest. Three barbs attached to his shirt, sinking through the flannel and into his flesh. To add insult to injury, Coy had then done the worst possible thing. He had jumped back, causing the barbs to rake deeply into his flesh as they attempted to hold on to their target.

Growing up on the ranch, he had suffered more than a few scrapes with wire. So it wasn't the pain that made him so angry; it was his own stupidity and carelessness. He had been working with half a mind, and he had reacted by instinct instead of thinking through what should have been done. If any of his ranch hands had done what he did, he would have blistered their hides with a lecture over their carelessness. Now everyone would know he, the owner, had been as careless as a greenhorn. And there was no way to hide his carelessness because he was now dripping copious amounts of blood from three large gashes on his chest.

Determinedly, he forced his mind to his task, being overly cautious so as to avoid another embarrassing injury. It took him longer than usual to fix the fence so by the time he was finished, Josh and Tanner had finished their section and made their way down to him.

"What did you do?" Josh asked, his tone accusing. Beside him, Tanner pressed his lips together and tried not to laugh.

"Something stupid," Coy snapped. The only way left to salvage this day was to go back to the ranch and try to make it to his room unseen by any of the other men. Not that Tanner wouldn't spread the story of his stupidity to everyone else. But maybe if they didn't see it for themselves, they would forget to give him a hard time over his ineptitude.

"I'm going back," he announced.

"You going to have a doctor take a look at that?" Tanner asked, trying hard not to laugh. "You might need stitches."

Josh laughed. "You should take the rest of the day off and maybe tomorrow, too. Go put your feet up."

"Hilarious," Coy said. He expected nothing less than their sarcastic teasing. Not only had he been monumentally stupid by allowing himself to be cut, but the cuts were far less serious than many injuries he and the other men had sustained over the years. And since there was so much testosterone running rampant on the ranch, there was little sympathy for the sight of blood. A wound had to be life threatening to faze any cowboy worth his salt.

He wanted to throw his tools in his saddlebag to relieve some of his pent up anger, but that might hurt his horse. No need to compound his idiocy by injuring an innocent animal. Instead, he forced himself to gently tuck his tools into his bag before mounting up and heading for the ranch at a run.

"I hope you don't mind running," he told his horse. "But I need to burn off some bad feelings."

The horse didn't answer, and Coy took that as a sign of her agreement.

By the time he arrived home, he was feeling much better. The cool wind had numbed the stinging pain in his chest and also helped to chill his hot temper. He was still vaguely annoyed at the interruption in his workday, but as soon as he got cleaned up, he would find something else to do. Maybe he could chip away at the never-ending paperwork Cade and Cam were always complaining about.

As if thinking Cam's name had caused him to appear, Coy saw his brother and Ivy entering the yard from the opposite side. She cut a fine figure sitting proudly in her fancy English saddle. His appreciation grew when she dismounted the horse while it was still mid-stride. It took an experienced rider to be able to do that, especially because the horse had been almost trotting.

His admiration turned to speculation when she jumped lightly off the horse and took off running. Where was she going? With a jolt, he realized she was headed for him.

"What happened to you?" she yelled when she was within shouting distance.

He looked down at his shirt and saw it covered in blood. "It's only some scratches."

She stopped short and stared up at him. "Some scratches? My lands. Did you wrestle a grizzly?"

He smiled, both at her concern and her charming turn of phrase. Could she be any more adorable? Coy didn't think it was possible. "Wrestling a bear would have been a much more respectable story. No, I wrestled a wire fence. The fence won. I don't want a rematch."

"Is it a few scratches, really? There's so much blood." She bit her lip worriedly and looked at him, her big blue eyes rounded with concern.

Coy realized then why men willingly went to war; it was because there was the possibility of some woman waiting for them with this expression on her face. After years of callous disregard by the other men on the ranch, he had almost forgotten how good it felt to be fussed over by a woman.

"I'm okay, really," he said softly. Cam reached them, looking imperious from his superior height on the horse as well as from his mocking expression.

"What'd you do?" he asked knowingly.

"Fence," Coy said, his tone clipped.

"I've heard those fences are mean. Use your gun next time."

Ivy frowned and tried to hold her tongue. She knew it would be worse for Coy if she tried to stand up for him, but she would never enjoy the way men interacted with each other when one of them was injured. What was so wrong with showing some sympathy?

Her brothers were the same way. They had laughed when she fell in a hornet's nest and received a dozen painful stings. But then there had been one time when she fell off her horse and broke her arm. Her brother had carried her two miles, talking gently the whole way. In the male mind, there was some line of demarcation about how an injury should rank by level of sympathy it should receive. She had no idea what that line was; apparently she lacked the testosterone to tell the difference. To her, all injuries deserved a little TLC. With that thought in mind, she turned her attention back to Coy.

"Let me put my horse away and I'll help you get cleaned up," she said. Perhaps she should have felt awkward making the suggestion in front of Cam, but she didn't. She would have done the same for any man who was in need of care. Maybe she wouldn't enjoy the prospect as much for someone else, but she tried not to think about that.

"I'll take care of the horses," Cam offered. "Take pumpkin to the house and give him a sucker when he's done."

Coy dismounted and tossed his reins to Cam's outstretched hand. "I'm going to eat all the suckers, and I'm not going to save any for you," he said.

Cam laughed and turned the horses toward the barn.

"Men," Ivy huffed.

Coy turned to smile at her. "What about men?"

"You're all crazy," she said.

He laughed. His first instinct was to drape his arm over her shoulders as they walked side by side to the house, but he refrained. When they reached the kitchen, Layla turned and dropped a pan at the sight of him. Her reaction, while gratifying, didn't have the same effect as Ivy's worry.

"It's some scratches," he said.

Layla and Ivy shared a look. Layla shook her head. "Men."

"That's what I said," Ivy said.

"Here you go." Layla bent, reached inside a cabinet, and retrieved a metal first aid kit. "I put this together as soon as I realized how many wounds I would end up doctoring. You would think we live in a war zone with the amount of blood I've seen. Truthfully, I'm glad to have a break from dressing wounds. Contrary to how much of it I've had to clean up, I don't actually enjoy the sight of blood." With one last grimace at Coy, she left the room, her long hair swishing behind her.

"Well, she told me," Coy said.

Ivy smiled. "I like her. She's sweet."

"I feel the same way," Coy said. "You can't imagine what it was like with Cade before she came along. After the accident, he was wasting away both in body and soul. Layla brought a spark back to him and pulled him out of wherever he was."

"It's something to see the love between them," she said.

"It is," he said with a faraway look. She wondered if watching Layla and Cade made him feel as wistful as she had felt when she saw them together. Then he answered her unasked question. "There's something about that kind of love that makes me want it for myself." He raised his eyes to her and she froze with her hand in the medical kit.

"I think it hits everyone that way," she said, striving for a casual tone.

"I suppose you're right. Look what it did for Cam." He dropped his eyes to his shirt and began unbuttoning while Ivy frowned at the bandages in her hand.

Was that what Cam's invitation had been about? They had been talking for a while and then all of a sudden he invited her to the ranch.

What had felt like a whim was beginning to make sense. Layla's arrival apparently had Coy and Cam thinking about their futures.

Coy finished unbuttoning his shirt. He took it off and set it aside. Ivy picked it up to inspect it. There were three large gashes in the front and it was soaked with blood. "I'm afraid this shirt is done for."

"We go through a lot of clothes here," Coy said. "I always feel a little bad we don't have much to donate to charity, but by the time we get through with clothes they're pretty much totaled."

"I don't doubt it," she said. Absently, she set the shirt aside and turned to inspect him. "Oh, Coy, what did you do to yourself? This looks horrible." She leaned close to inspect his cuts. He closed his eyes, inhaling her sweet scent. He was so tired of the smell of leather, horse manure, and sweat. It was heavenly to be near a soft, pretty, and good-smelling girl.

"I like your perfume," he said, his voice embarrassingly hoarse.

"I'll buy you some for Christmas," she said lightly, causing him to laugh. "It's going to sting when I clean these wounds."

"I'm not sure it could sting any more than it already does," he said, but he was wrong. The wounds had settled down to a dull ache, but with the addition of liquid and the touch of her hand they woke up again and flamed like fire. Still, he didn't wince. He had emasculated himself enough for one day. No need to add to the girlish picture he was presenting.

Ivy, irritated by his stoicism, paused in her ministrations to retrieve some pain reliever for him. She held a couple of pills out to him, along with a glass of water.

"No, thank you. I'm fine," Coy said.

She shoved them farther under his nose. "I'll open your gullet and shove them down if I have to. Do you really think I'm going to tell the other men you took pain reliever? Stop acting like Mr. Macho Cowboy and admit this hurts a little bit."

He took the pills, but made no such admission of pain.

"Men," she muttered again. Although she supposed she really wouldn't want it any other way. The differences between the sexes were what made them intriguing to each other. No doubt if Coy started to cry and whine about the horrible pain he must be in, she would be repulsed by his weakness. Women, she realized, were as irritating as men sometimes. "And women," she added.

"Amen to that," Coy said.

"You're not allowed to agree with me," she said.

"First you wanted me to be quiet and take the pills, then you said I'm not allowed to agree with you. I'm not sure you know what you want."

That was certainly true. Since her thoughts were much deeper than his, she remained silent while she slathered his wounds with antibacterial cream before taping them with bandages.

"You're a good nurse," he said. Like Layla, she was gentle and efficient as she worked over him.

"I've had a lot of practice on my brothers. They're always getting themselves hurt and then suddenly they're glad I'm a girl and can put them back together."

"It would have been nice to have a sister," he said.

"Yes, it would have," she agreed.

"If you marry Cam, you would be my sister."

Her hand stilled on the bandages. "I suppose that's so. That first night when we slept in the truck, I tried to pretend you were my brother so things wouldn't feel so awkward."

"Did it work?" he asked.

She paused again before answering. "No."

There was an awkward lull in conversation. Coy tried to think of some way, any way to fill the silence. "Layla feels like a real sister to me. At first when she arrived here, I was interested in her. But once I realized she was for Cade, I was amazed at how easy it was to think sisterly thoughts about her." He frowned, wishing he could do the same for Ivy.

"I think we're all done here," Ivy said. Using her fingers to seal the edge of the bandages, she stood back to admire her handiwork, inadvertently admiring his physique in the process. He was more compact and less hairy than her brothers who all looked like Yetis as far as she was concerned. In fact, they could easily be mistaken for the missing link from far away.

"Did I tell you about the time my brothers faked a Bigfoot video and sent it to a tabloid?" she asked.

Coy began to laugh, and then laughed harder as she regaled him with the outrageous story. They lost track of time as they sat in the kitchen talking and laughing together until it was eventually time for supper. Even when Layla entered and began preparing food, they took no notice of her, so lost were they in their own little world.

CHAPTER 16

Cam wasn't finished with the surprises he had in store for Ivy. The next day, he invited her to a dance.

"A dance?" Coy repeated, trying to figure out when his brother had suddenly turned into a sophisticated charmer who had expensive saddles made and invited girls to go dancing. It was as if he was reading a book called, *How to Woo a Girl in Ten Easy Steps*, or something. Where was he coming up with this stuff? And, more importantly, was it working?

"A dance sounds fun," Ivy said. She sounded sincere.

Of course she did, Coy thought. What girl didn't enjoy dancing? "Can I come?" he found himself asking, hoping he didn't sound as pathetic to everyone else as he did to himself.

Cam shot him a disbelieving glance. "Do you have a date?"

Coy searched his mind, trying to come up with someone he could bring at the last minute. "No," he said lamely. "Maybe I'll meet someone there." To cover the awkwardness his question had caused, he glanced around the table. "Let's all go."

"Dancing and wheelchairs don't exactly go hand in hand. You can take Layla if you want," Cade said, trying not to sound reluctant. He was always loathe to have his wheelchair hold Layla back from anything she might want to do. And he always put too much importance on things that held no meaning to Layla.

"Stop trying to pawn me off on people. Why would I want to go without you?" she asked. "We'll have our own dance." By the way she winked and gave Cade a secret smile Coy guessed "dance" was code for "extended makeout session."

"Josh?" Coy turned to his youngest brother. "How about it? You'd have to touch a girl, but I promise it would be worth it."

Josh scowled at him. "I've danced with plenty of girls, thank you very much. But Nikita has been sick the last couple of days, and I don't want to leave her. I think maybe she ate something bad. If she's not better by tomorrow, I'm calling the vet."

Nikita was his dog. Secretly and behind his back, the other brothers referred to her as Josh's girlfriend because he spent a lot of time with her and lavished all his care and attention on her. Rarely had someone been more devoted to a dog.

Coy knew at this point he should give in and let Cam and Ivy go by themselves. To keep pursuing his spot as a third wheel would be awkward and pathetic. "So what time do we need to leave?" he asked.

Cade put his hand over his eyes and shook his head.

* * *

IT WAS WORSE than his worst nightmare, Coy thought. He sat in the backseat unabashedly eavesdropping on Cam and Ivy's conversation while staring at Ivy and resisting the urge to reach out and touch her.

Her hair was in a loose chignon with several strands falling softly around her face and neck. The dress fit her perfectly, highlighting her willowy, graceful figure. She was beautiful. She was perfect. She wasn't his.

That fact became painfully clear when they arrived at the dance and Cam immediately whisked her away for a slow dance. Coy stood on the sidelines, not even attempting to look for another girl to dance with.

"Don't tell me you're dateless."

Coy turned to see a man he had known almost all his life. "Dobbie. What are you doing here?" He was a foreman on a ranch the next county over. Coy had seen him at various ranching events over the years, but they hadn't become friends until Coy was thirteen and showed a cow at the state fair. Dobbie was there as the winner from his county and, although he was two years older, the two boys had become friends. Despite having known him for years, Coy had never heard anyone call him anything other than Dobbie.

"My wife has been hinting she needs some 'culture.'" He used his fingers to make air quotes. "Usually that means I have to take her to the theater in Billings, but they're playing something I can't pronounce. So I brought her dancing."

"Wow, you are *whipped*," Coy said.

Dobbie smiled. "I have a beautiful wife who cooks for me. Pity me if you must. By the way, where did you say your date was?" He pretended to search the crowd.

Coy winced. "Ouch. Good point. I'm here with Cam and his girl."

"Cam found a girl? I mean, no, there's no way I can pretend I'm not surprised. Cam found a girl? What's she like?"

"She's sweet, pretty, funny, athletic, smart. She's some kind of super-genius with horses, and she has the cutest accent you've ever heard." He glanced at Cam and Ivy as they sashayed around the dance floor. Beside him Dobbie coughed, but it sounded suspiciously like a laugh.

"You laughing at me?" Coy asked him.

"I'm laughing at both of us. I married my ex-girlfriend's sister, and you're in love with your twin's girl. We're not exactly doing our part to dispel the notion of the inbred Montana cowboy."

"She's from Kentucky. That's not inbred," Coy protested. "Not like some sad people who marry their neighbors. Where is your wife, by the way?"

"She found the owner of your grocery store and she's convincing him to sell her jam."

"Mr. Landry is sort of a savvy businessman. Maybe you'd better go check on her," Coy suggested.

Dobbie laughed. "You don't know Libby. I should probably go check on Mr. Landry."

Just then Dobbie's wife, Libby, approached them. Coy had to admire Dobby's taste. Libby was a pretty brunette with soft brown eyes and long lashes. Every time Coy had seen her, she had a sweet smile on her face, and she barely reached midway to Dobbie's chest. Surely he was exaggerating about her salesmanship; she looked harmless.

"It's Coy, right?" she asked, extending her hand to him.

Coy took it and realized it wasn't held at an angle like a man; it was tipped delicately in an old-fashioned courtly gesture. He had the sudden urge to kiss her proffered hand and bow. Instead, he squeezed it lightly and smiled. "Nice to see you again, Libby. How did it go with Mr. Landry?"

She smiled. "He's going to sell my jam without taking a commission."

Coy and Dobbie made small talk about their ranches until Coy noticed Libby's wistful glances toward the dance floor.

"You guys should go dance," he suggested.

"I would offer you a dance with Libby, but I have a strict policy of never letting her dance with anyone under a hundred," Dobbie said.

"Wow, possessive much, Dobbie?" Coy teased, sharing a smile with a chagrined Libby.

"Have you seen her?" Dobbie pointed to Libby. "All the time. Every minute. And, hey, all's fair in love and war." He nodded his head in the direction of Cam and Ivy.

"Even among brothers?" Coy asked, desperate for advice or approval.

"Brothers or sisters. The heart wants what it wants. Things have a way of working themselves out. Trust me; I speak from experience."

"Thanks," Coy said as they walked away. "Hey, Libby," he called.

She paused and looked over her shoulder at him with a smile.

"What's Dobbie's real name?"

"It's…" she began, but Dobbie tugged her hand to drag her away.

"Don't dispel my mystique, Lib."

Coy smiled as he watched them sway gently together on the dance floor. He was glad Dobbie had found a happy ending. After losing his parents in a fire and then having his longtime girlfriend, Libby's sister, run off with another man, his life had seemed destined for tragedy. Now he practically oozed happiness and contentment, making Coy more than a little envious.

It was the same way with Cade. Apparently when love hit hard, it had the ability to change a man profoundly. Coy wanted that for himself, and the realization gave him pause. Was that what this was about with Ivy? Was he suddenly so desperate to find someone he turned to the first girl who was handy?

Cam and Ivy left the dance floor and made their way toward him. "Why don't you dance with Ivy for a while?" Cam asked. "Mr. Landry snagged my attention and said he needs to talk to me about something."

"Don't buy any jam; I can cut out the middleman for you," Coy said.

"Huh?" Cam asked.

"Never mind."

Cam left them to talk to Mr. Landry who was a chatty man and would probably keep him busy for some time.

"Would you like to dance?" Coy asked, sounding as nervous as he felt. He had danced with girls before; why was this different?

"Okay," Ivy replied, sounding equally as nervous.

A slow song was playing when he took her in his arms, and he suddenly understood his reticence from a few minutes ago. Holding her this way, it was no longer possible to deny his feelings for her. He wasn't simply attracted to her; he was in love with her. She fit him in every way, and he wanted her to stay exactly as she was for the rest of their lives. For the first time in his life he felt ruthless and willing to do whatever needed to be done to make her his, even if that meant cutting his brother out of the picture.

"Ivy," he said softly, unknowingly cinching her slightly closer when he said her name.

"Yes?" she whispered, blue eyes luminous as she stared pensively up at him.

"Do you believe all's fair in love and war?"

CHAPTER 17

Ivy never got the chance to answer Coy's impromptu question. Just then, Cam returned to claim her.

"Mr. Landry really did want to talk to me about jam. He said Dobbie's wife mesmerized him into making some sort of deal where he wouldn't make any money from her jam for a year. He wanted me to talk to Dobbie and get him out of it. I told him you were the one who is friends with Dobbie, so be on the lookout. I also told him it wasn't very honorable to renege on a deal, especially not with a girl." He glanced at Dobbie and Libby. "How did he get taken in by her? She's such a little thing."

"Maybe that's part of her charm. She seems harmless and then she goes in for the kill," Ivy suggested. "Women have to use any advantage we can to get ahead. It's a man's world."

Instead of dancing together again, Ivy and Cam began a debate about ethical business practices that lasted the rest of the evening. Coy was content to listen to them spar with each other. It helped cover his guilty conscience. How could he have thought about betraying his brother, even for a moment?

Holding Ivy in his arms had confused his senses. He needed to get some space from her; he needed to think.

* * *

But finding space seemed impossible, even on a ranch as vast as theirs. After sitting mum in the back seat on the ride home the night before, Coy left early the next morning and spent the day working on his own, fulfilling various projects that had been on his to-do list for a long time.

There was no good reason to skip supper, but after he ate he planned to go to town. Maybe he would see a movie, even if it meant he had to sit alone in the theater. His brother, however, had other plans.

"Ivy wants to play ball after supper," Cam announced. "Who's in?"

"I'll sit this one out," Cade said wryly.

"You could play," Ivy said.

"I could," Cade conceded. "But it would be easier if I didn't, and I'm not really up for it tonight anyway. Maybe some other time."

"I'm in," Josh said. Josh was the most sports-minded of all the brothers. He played football and baseball for his high school. He would have played basketball, but the roads were too iffy to commit to a sport during the winter.

"We need a fourth," Cam said, turning to Coy. Was he purposely trying to torture him?

"Please?" Ivy said. Her crystal-blue eyes somehow managed to look warm and soft despite their icy color.

"Okay," Coy found himself agreeing. Despite the chilly October temperatures, he changed into shorts and a t-shirt before heading to their basketball court. Actually, it was a basketball hoop in a flat pasture they kept mowed low—not exactly the ideal playing space. But since their father retired and Cade became injured, they had little time for extracurricular activities like playing ball. Nowadays Josh was the only one who used this space, and Coy realized how much he missed playing as soon as he saw the familiar rim in the distance.

"How about you and Josh on a team and spot us a few points," Cam suggested quietly, but not quietly enough. Ivy stood from where she had been tying her shoe, looking mutinous.

"How about I'll take Josh and we'll give you guys a handicap?"

Josh liked that idea, and there was no way Cam could disagree without wounding her pride again. And when they started to play, he wished he had kept his mouth shut altogether. Though he and Coy had dominated on the field as high school football players, neither of them had ever excelled at basketball. Unfortunately for them, Ivy had. She was good, better than good; she was amazing.

Not only was she fast and an accurate shot, but she was fearless. If they had a referee, he probably would have called foul on her numerous times for the forceful body checks she performed on Cam and Coy. But since both of them were too proud to complain over being roughed up by a girl, she got away with it, which was probably part of her strategy.

After winning two games in a row, she and Josh spent a long time enthusiastically high-fiving each other while Cam and Coy bent over, trying to catch their breath.

"I would say you guys are getting too old for this sort of thing, but since I'm a few months older than you I guess that's not why you lost," Ivy said.

"Wow, you're a horrible winner," Coy said, wheezing a little from the asthma that only showed up when he was getting a hard workout.

Cam remained stoic, his frown saying more than any words could have. He hated to lose, especially to a girl. Coy was impressed with his reserve because if a man had played as roughly as Ivy had, Cam probably would have belted him. He hadn't said a word to Ivy, but Coy could tell he was irritated with her. Coy, on the other hand, was amused someone so pretty could also be so ruthless.

"I'm going to shower," Cam said, heading to the house.

"He's mad at me, huh?" Ivy asked. She and Coy sat on the grass while Josh picked up the ball and began shooting.

"He doesn't like to lose so badly," Coy said.

"He shouldn't have said that about spotting me some points. He knows I played ball in college," she said irritably, plucking a blade of grass before tossing it away.

"He was trying to be nice," Coy said, feeling caught in the middle between them.

"You're taking his side?" she asked.

"It's a stupid game of basketball; there are no sides," he said.

She blew out a breath. "You're right. I'm overreacting. I don't know what's wrong with me." But she did know what was wrong with her; she was horribly confused, more than she had ever been. Last night at the dance, she'd had a good time with Cam. He had been pleasant company, and he was a surprisingly good dancer. But that was it. There was no passion between them. Previously, she had no idea passion was important to her. And then she met Coy.

She felt like she had to decide between doing the right thing by sticking with the ever sensible Cam or going with her crazy whim to find passion with Coy. The rational part of her brain, the part she had always listened to before, was telling her Cam was the right choice. She knew him. They had a history together. They had spent an entire year cultivating a solid friendship together. On paper, they were perfect for each other.

But her heart was difficult to ignore as it reminded her of all the sweet, funny, and tender things Coy had said and done since she met him. He had taken care of her during a dire emergency. What better indicator was there of a man's true character than the decisions he made during a life and death situation? Coy had unfailingly put her first, even taking a potentially fatal hit in order to spare her life. Then, despite being injured, he had put her well-being and comfort ahead of his own, always making sure she ate and kept warm. And he had been cheerful throughout their ordeal. There was also the awkward reality of her physical reaction to him. If she closed her eyes, she could still imagine the way his arms had felt around her, and the sensation gave her goosebumps. There were no goosebumps when she was near Cam, but were they enough to base her future on? That chemical physical reaction would fade over time, wouldn't it? How important was it now? Wasn't friendship more important?

"I think the temperature has dropped ten degrees since we've been out here," Coy said. His finger brushed down her arm. "You have goosebumps. Let's get you inside before you catch your death."

They returned to the house where Layla and Cade were waiting to hear the results of the game. Cam sat at the kitchen table, his hair wet, and his expression grim.

"Ivy and Josh won," he said as Ivy and Coy entered the room.

"I sort of cheated," Ivy admitted. "I knew none of you would call me on my over-the-top fouls. Sorry." She gave Cam a tentative and sheepish smile which he returned.

"Don't worry about it," he said. "For a minute, it was a little like being in the NBA."

Now it was Coy's turn to look sullen as Cam and Ivy recounted the highlights of the game for Cade and Layla. He should shower. He should do anything but sit here and yearn for things that were out of his reach, but like an addict who can't give up what's bad for him, he remained seated, staring at Ivy and wishing she were his.

* * *

Ivy woke with a start. She had been so certain if she got in a good workout, she would be able to sleep. At first, her theory appeared to work. After showering, she had crawled between the sheets and fallen asleep without first checking the empty space beside her. But then she woke up less than two hours later and remained wide awake.

Her sleeplessness since the accident was only adding to her anxiety and confusion. How was she supposed to think clearly if she didn't sleep? But how was she supposed to sleep when the space beside her felt strangely empty? Every time she finally fell asleep, she woke a short time later, her hand frantically sifting the space beside her. No doubt about it; she was losing her mind.

The minutes ticked as she lay staring at the ceiling, willing herself to go back to sleep. Her thoughts turned to the hot cocoa Layla had made for them that evening. There was some leftover, and it was in the fridge, calling Ivy's name. Maybe if she rose and reheated it the warm milk might help her fall back asleep. Wasn't warm milk the cure-all for sleeplessness before the invention of modern medicine? Whether it was or wasn't, it sounded good to Ivy.

Stealthily, she crept out of bed and stole down the long hallway to the kitchen. It took a few minutes to fumble for the lights. She froze and doubled over when she kicked a chair and stubbed her toe. The soft noise was apparently too soft to disturb anyone else in the house, so she finished scurrying around, re-warming the cocoa in the microwave.

The kitchen felt hollow and cold with no one else to occupy the cavernous space. Ivy decided to take her drink into the living room and curl up in one of the comfortable-looking chairs by the fireplace. Even though there was no fire, it still radiated coziness.

She sipped at the cocoa on her journey to the living room, finding it the right temperature. There was something pleasant about being the only one awake on this isolated ranch. In a way, she felt like the only person in the world, a novelty after living for so long with five older brothers. Though their horse farm was large by Kentucky standards, it resembled someone's back yard compared to the King's vast spread. She found she rather liked the sprawling space and wondered if home would feel cramped now.

Before she could settle in a wing chair, the sight outside the window caught her interest, drawing her forward. It was snowing, giant, fluffy flakes that landed gently on the earth before rising again to blow and drift. It must have been snowing for some time because there was already a light layer of white on the ground. The moon was full, illuminating the spectacular show, and Ivy was mesmerized.

"Beautiful, isn't it?"

Thankfully, she didn't jump or scream when the voice whispered from the couch behind her. She simply turned to look at him.

"Sorry, did I scare you?" Coy asked. "I couldn't tell if you saw me or not."

"I don't know how I could have missed you," she said. She had passed the couch on her way to the window, but she had been intent on the breathtaking scene outside. "Couldn't sleep?" she asked.

He shook his head. "What are you drinking?"

"Cocoa. Want some?" She held out her cup to him.

He nodded and she walked forward until the cup was in reach. He took a hefty gulp and handed it back. "Thanks," he said.

For lack of a reply, she turned back to the window. "I much prefer to watch this from the safety of the house," she said, thinking of their time stuck in the snow.

"It was cold in the truck, but it was pretty. I woke a while before you did and watched it snow for a long time." With a pang, he remembered how it had felt that morning to hold her in his arms as the snow fell outside. At the time, he hadn't been able to put a name to what he had been feeling. Now he knew it was contentment. Despite his injury and the peril of their situation, he could have stayed like that forever.

She took another sip of the cocoa and handed the mug to him. "Finish it, please. It's growing cold."

He took the cup from her and drained it. "Thanks." He set it on the table beside him.

"I guess I should get back to bed," she said to fill the awkward silence. Coy made no reply, so she took a step toward her bedroom. His hand shot out to grasp her wrist, holding her back.

"Stay," he said, his voice rough with some unknown emotion.

Ivy swallowed and glanced down the hall. She shouldn't give in to his request, or command, or whatever it had been. She should do the sensible thing, the right thing, and go to bed. Maybe if she simply sat beside him a few minutes, they could have a rational conversation like the two mature adults they were.

Tentatively, she sat beside him on the couch, a few inches away and not touching. But Coy had other ideas. He picked her up as if she weighed nothing at all, wrapped a quilt around both of them, and held her tightly against his chest. And Ivy said not a word of protest. Instead, she laid her head on his shoulder and stared out the window, watching the pretty snowflakes fall. Five minutes later, she was asleep.

ayla Smith woke with a smile, as she did on most days. Her boyfriend, Cade, accused her of being an optimist, and maybe she was. All she knew was she had a lot to smile about these days, especially in the mornings. The mornings were hers. She made a habit of waking a few minutes before Cade or his brothers so she could have her alone time with her first cup of coffee. It was a peaceful routine she guarded somewhat jealously.

For that reason when she left her room and noticed a shape on the couch, her smile turned to a frown. Who was up? Was someone sick? Was it Cade? No, she assured herself. After so long together, Cade would have woken her to take care of him rather than risk her wrath for suffering alone.

She really needed to have her eyes checked, she thought as she squinted to distinguish the shape. As she drew closer, the curly hair alerted her to the fact that it was Coy. Her heart softened with the realization. Coy hadn't been sleeping well since Ivy arrived. If Ivy's copious coffee consumption throughout the day was any indication, she hadn't been sleeping well, either. Layla felt sorry for both of them. They were stuck in a no-win situation, rife with emotional minefields.

But as she crept close enough to touch Coy, her feelings turned to dismay. Coy wasn't alone; Ivy was in his arms. They were both asleep, looking very much like two halves of a whole that had finally come together.

Layla's hand remained outstretched in midair, hovering uncertainly. She really did not want to involve herself in this situation. Was there any way to wake them without revealing she had caught them cuddled in such an intimate embrace? A sound from behind her alerted her to the fact that Cam was stirring. He was always the first brother awake, usually followed by Josh, Coy, and then her sleepyhead Cade. She couldn't allow Cam to walk in and witness this scene; that would be horrible for all concerned. Better to bite the bullet and immerse herself into the awkwardness if it meant sparing Cam.

"Coy, Ivy," Layla whispered, shaking Coy's shoulder.

"Hmm," he replied sleepily, drawing Ivy closer. In turn, Ivy burrowed her face in Coy's shoulder and snuggled closer.

"Oh, dear," Layla said, starting to panic now. What if she couldn't get them to wake up? What if Cam saw them this way? She knew the fight that had ensued between Cade and his brothers when she went away. How much worse would it be this time?

"Coy," she whispered louder and shook him harder. "Ivy." For good measure, she shook Ivy's shoulder, too.

Ivy was the first to wake. Smiling, she looked up at Coy. Then her smile quickly froze and fell away to be replaced by mortification when she saw Layla looming over them.

"Oh," she said. Clapping her hand over her mouth to stifle the sound, she stood and sprinted down the hall, her cheeks cherry red from embarrassment.

Coy wiped his hand down his face and gave Layla a look of chagrin.

"Not good," she said. "Not good at all, Coy."

"Tell me about it," he muttered, feeling some embarrassment of his own. What had he been thinking? He hadn't, and that was the problem. After lying in bed a sleepless hour, he had finally come out to the couch for a change of scenery. But he hadn't been able to enjoy the view because all thoughts were on Ivy. Then, as if thinking about her somehow caused her to appear, she was standing in front of him in a silky white nightgown, sipping something from a mug. Her pretty blond hair had been long and loose down her back and at that moment all rational thought had gone out the window. He only knew he wanted, no, *needed* to touch her, to hold her.

But he certainly hadn't meant to sleep with her in his arms for three hours. What if Cam had been the one to discover them? Or even worse Josh, who felt it his duty to report all the happenings at the ranch—especially the bad ones—to their mother. He had been stupid and irresponsible. What happened to his vow to gain some distance? Pulling her into his lap had been the opposite of finding distance.

He turned to ask Layla's advice, but she was already gone. Instead, he encountered Cam, staring at him with a concerned expression.

"You sick?" Cam asked.

Coy's gut twisted with guilt, making him irritable. "No." He stood and threw off the quilt before stalking down the hall to his room to dress for the day. Skipping breakfast would make him even more irritable, but it couldn't be helped. There was no way he could take one more day of sitting across from Ivy, pretending there was nothing between them. He had to get away, had to find a distraction.

Fortunately, a distraction arrived as he was walking to his truck.

"Hey, Coy, going somewhere?"

Coy closed the door of his truck and smiled at the newcomer. "Hey, PJ." He looked behind the girl to see her father's truck parked in front of the horse barn. Her father, Joseph, had been their farrier for as long as Coy could remember, trimming their horses' hooves every few weeks. And every time he arrived at the ranch, PJ arrived in tow. She was a cute seventeen-year-old tomboy with a ponytail and plucky attitude. If the way she adoringly followed Coy around the ranch was any indication, she also had a crush on him. She was a young seventeen, too girlish and inexperienced to appeal to Coy, but he found her endearing, and her attention flattering. Today, especially, he could use the pick-me-up PJ provided, as well as the ego boost.

"You didn't answer my question. Are you going somewhere?" she asked. Her mother was a full-blooded Native American, gifting PJ with big, beautiful black eyes and long lashes.

Coy stood debating a minute. PJ always provided amusement when she showed up; with her here, he had no need to flee as if hounds were chasing him. "No, I'm not going anywhere. But I do have a tractor that's broken. Want to take a look?"

"You mean it?" she asked eagerly, her ponytail practically quivering with anticipation.

"Sure I do," Coy said. "This way." He pointed toward the back of the equipment barn where the tractors were kept.

"What's wrong with it?" she asked, propping her hands on the seat and standing on her toes to try and see everything at once.

"The starter is locked," Coy said. "Can you fix it?"

"Sure I can," she said. "But I'll need your help. I'm going to put it in the highest gear." She paused to jump into the seat, depress the clutch, and switch gears. Refusing Coy's help, she hopped down and brushed the seat of her pants. "Now we rock it." She braced herself on one side while he stood next to the other tall tire, and they rocked the tractor back and forth. A couple of years ago, he would have made fun of her unconventional technique, but she had proved her salt so often he no longer doubted her wisdom when it came to tractors. She had single-handedly saved them a bundle in repairs since she took up engine repair as a hobby.

"Okay, try," she said, wiping her brow with the edge of her sleeve.

Coy jumped into the seat, cranked the motor, and smiled when it purred to life. "PJ, you're a genius."

She shuffled her toes and stared at them. "It was nothing." She raised her head, a look of alarm on her face. "You're not going to leave now, are you?"

"I was thinking maybe we could go for a ride, if you want," he suggested. Despite the fact that her father was a farrier, he lived in town and didn't own horses. PJ loved horses. If Coy wasn't busy when she showed up, he always tried to take a ride with her.

"Really?" she asked. Her bald enthusiasm was a sign of her inexperience. Most girls he knew were too smooth to wear their emotions on the sleeves.

"Really, really," he said. "You can choose your mount."

They walked side by side to the horse barn while PJ bobbed enthusiastically, using her hands for emphasis as she talked about what had been going on in her life. She was a year behind Josh in school, but she had always seemed much younger to Coy. Despite the smallness of the town's high school, she and Josh weren't friends. But then, Josh didn't believe in being friends with girls. He was friends with his teammates and his brothers, and that was it.

Coy saddled their horses while PJ continued her narrative. Her mindless chatter was exactly what his overworked brain and emotions needed. He smiled, trying to remember a time when he had been as carefree and lighthearted—had it only been two weeks ago his world was sunny and bright?

They rode for hours, talking about sports, cars, and people they both knew. For Coy, it was almost like taking a vacation. Not only was he not doing any work, but he was also able to suspend all thought and emotion by immersing himself in PJ's innocent teenage life.

When they both sensed PJ's father's workday would be coming to an end, they turned tail and headed for home. Coy dismounted while PJ remained seated, waiting for his help. As much as she loved horses, she didn't have a lot of experience with them. Though she would never admit it, she was somewhat frightened of them, although she preferred to pretend she wasn't afraid of anything.

Coy put his arms up to lift her down. When they were eye level, he was struck by the sudden desire to kiss her. He had kissed a lot of girls in his time, but never PJ. There were other girls like PJ who came to their ranch with their fathers, and Coy had kissed most of them at one time or another. What was most surprising was that he hadn't kissed PJ before now, especially because she had a crush on him. But now he saw himself as Ivy might see him—a spurious Casanova, taking what he could get with no thought to who he hurt, and he didn't like what he saw. The unexpected feeling came out of nowhere, leaving him stunned and vaguely ashamed.

In a rare moment of mature intuition, PJ seemed to read and understand his intention and subsequent hesitation. "Aren't you going to kiss me?" she asked, sounding half hopeful and half afraid.

"No, I'm not," he said gravely, letting her go and taking a step back.

"Why not?" she asked.

"I'm too old for you, PJ," he said, aiming for the easy answer.

"Four years isn't so much," she said, her lower lip jutting slightly in a pout.

"For us it is. Plus, your father works for us and trusts you with me. I can't take advantage of that." *Starting now,* he added. Previously, he hadn't given much thought to any of the reasons he had listed, but now that he did he felt a little nauseated at his past behavior.

"I wouldn't tell him," she said, mortified.

"But I would know. And there's someone else for me. You're very cute, and a lot of fun, but you're not for me, and I'm not for you. Save your kisses for someone who deserves them, and we'll keep on being friends." He smiled to soften his words. He didn't want to hurt her, but he also didn't want to leave her with the hope there could be a future for them.

"Can I still come here, work on your tractors, and ride?"

"Of course you can. We're friends."

"Okay." Her smile looked a little watery, but he thought she would be okay. Much better than if he had given in to temptation, kissed her, and left her heartbroken in his wake.

Her father called her a moment later. Usually Coy went over to exchange a few words with him, but today he remained in the barn, staring absently at his horse.

Somehow it was appropriate that passing on a kiss should mark his official entrance into adulthood. Previously if the temptation to kiss PJ had happened, he would have kissed her and possibly felt guilty later. The fact that he had thought before he acted was an indication of what falling in love had done to him.

No matter how things turned out with Ivy, Coy would remain

forever changed; there was no going back. Gone were the days when he could trample a girl's feelings and discard her without a care. Henceforth he would always picture that girl as Ivy and imagine how he would want her to be treated.

If he were being honest, he wasn't altogether happy with this new change in him. Nothing less than true devotion would cause him to give up his love 'em and leave 'em lifestyle. As far as he was concerned, he had found that with Ivy. But what about her? What did Ivy feel?

He sat in the barn a long time, absently picking apart pieces of hay and pondering his life.

CHAPTER 19

Currently what Ivy felt was mortification. Not only was she embarrassed she had given in to temptation and fell asleep on the couch with Coy, but then she had been discovered by Layla. How could she ever leave her bedroom again? How could she ever look any of them in the eye again after humiliating herself so completely?

She couldn't.

But she did have to leave her room; there was no getting around it. She would simply have to keep her head down and escape to the outdoors as soon as breakfast was over.

By the time she finally dredged up the courage to leave her room, breakfast was already in progress. That was good; slipping into the room unnoticed was her goal. For a few minutes everyone was quiet, and then Josh finished his food and spoke.

"Did you see Coy's girlfriend pull up outside?" Oblivious to the sudden tension at the table, he continued. "I don't know what girls see in him, but it must be something. He sure has enough of them trailing after him. And the weirder they are, the more they like him. Guys don't look twice at PJ at school, but then she comes here and Coy…"

Cam interrupted him. "Josh, enough. PJ is a perfectly nice girl, and I don't want to hear anything bad about her."

"She is nice," Josh agreed. "If you like that type. I like girls who look like girls, but obviously Coy doesn't share the sentiment."

"Josh," Cade added warningly.

"What?" Josh asked, oblivious. "It's not like everyone doesn't know PJ has a crush on him. And it's not like Coy is some saint who's not going to do something about it. I can only imagine what they do when they go riding together so often." He broke off his speech when Ivy stood.

"I think I'll take another look at the horses," she announced. Turning, she practically sprinted from the house.

"She sure likes horses," Josh said, staring after her.

Over the table, Cade and Layla shared a look. Cade rolled his eyes. Cam stared after Ivy, a thoughtful look on his face.

Ivy rounded the corner of the house and stopped to catch her breath. Was she losing her mind? Her first impression of Coy had been negative, but with three days of forced togetherness her opinion changed. Then they returned home and his family was doing their best to try and convince her that her original opinion was the correct one. What was true, and what was wishful thinking?

After a couple of deep breaths that did nothing to calm her inner emotional turmoil, she walked toward the horse barn. Horses always had the capacity to ease her anxiety and bring peace, no matter what she was going through. Maybe horses had that effect on everyone; they certainly worked to calm her brothers. Working with their horses was the only time she saw her brothers mature, calm, and professional, which is why she remained working in the family business. While they were at work, her brothers behaved themselves. If they didn't, Ivy would have chosen another profession and moved to a foreign country with no forwarding address.

She busied herself with the horses all day. The farrier was there, and she spent some time talking to him. He was good at his job, and it was pleasant to talk to someone else who cared about proper horse maintenance as much as she did. He had never traveled east of the Mississippi and was curious about Kentucky.

Unable to face the family any more that day, Ivy skipped lunch. Her blood sugar plummeted, causing her to feel weak and cranky, but after so many days without food, she was becoming used to the feeling. She looked toward the copse of trees in the distance, vaguely wondering if there were any limber pines whose cones she could filch. Then, remembering how much sap had gotten on her hands and how difficult it had been to remove, she quickly dismissed that idea.

Two hours later, she couldn't take it anymore. Her brain felt foggy and her hands were shaking. She would sneak into the kitchen for a snack and hopefully she wouldn't run into anyone on her way.

She felt like a thief as she tiptoed into the kitchen. Some cookies Layla had baked were sitting on the counter. Ivy opened the container and stuck her hand in when a voice spoke from behind her.

"I literally caught you with your hand in the cookie jar," Cam said. He lounged in the doorway, his shoulder touching the beam.

"I'm hungry," she explained unnecessarily. Of course she was hungry, why else would she be eating?

"I didn't see you at lunch," Cam said. He tipped his head to the side. "In fact, I haven't seen you since breakfast this morning."

Ivy shrugged, trying to look nonchalant. "I wanted to spend some time getting to know the horses."

Cam didn't respond to that at first. She wondered if the comment had been too presumptuous. Things between them weren't going well; why should she believe she had a future with the horses if she didn't have a future with this man?

"I have some things I need to take care of in the office for the rest of the day. But I'd like to ride with you tomorrow morning. Are you available?"

"Of course," she answered. "Riding sounds nice." She smiled to try and make her words believable. At this point, she didn't want to ride with Cam. She wanted to closet herself in her room with a dozen of Layla's cookies, cry, and feel sorry for herself over the horrible vacation this had turned out to be.

"Okay," Cam said. He stared at her a few beats longer before turning and exiting the kitchen.

Ivy stuffed three cookies in her mouth, then put her hand up to catch crumbs while she chewed the giant mouthful. Only the thought of what someone would say if they realized she was the culprit kept her from devouring the remaining dozen cookies.

Since there were still two more hours until supper, she decided to spend some more quality time with the horses. One in particular was favoring an ankle, and she wanted to massage some liniment into it to see if it might help. But when she exited the house, she stopped short and ducked behind the porch beam. Coy was helping a cute young girl off a horse and from their intimate position, Ivy was positive they were about to kiss.

She slid around the beam, faced the house, and squeezed her eyes shut. She didn't want to see. She didn't want to know how wrong she had been about him. From what Josh had said, the girl was still a kid. What kind of man went around preying on the affections of a child? Not any kind of man she wanted, that was for sure.

Really, she should feel relieved. Coy was making her decision easy by taking himself out of the running. Without him in the picture, there was only Cam. Maybe tomorrow she and Cam could make a real start of things. With no one else between them, surely the chemistry would have a chance to develop.

She had no idea she was marching toward the horse barn until she reached it, and then she was inside and it was too late to stop.

"Ivy," Coy said, looking up at her in surprise.

No, his eyes didn't light at the sight of you. It's a trick; stop the nonsense and get it over with. "Did you have a nice ride?" she asked.

He shrugged and stared at the piece of straw between his fingers. "It was okay. She's a nice kid."

He sat on the ground in front of her while she stood towering over him, frowning at the top of his Stetson. He admitted the girl was a child, and yet he still kissed her. Unbelievable.

When he looked up at her, her resolve wavered. How did he manage to look so innocent and attractive at the same time?

"Ivy, we need to talk," he said, tossing the mangled piece of straw away.

"We do," she agreed.

He blew out a breath. "The thing is, I've dated a lot of girls and…"

Whatever weakness he had almost created in her was gone as soon as he reminded her of the other girls. She held up a hand to cut him off. "You don't have to explain anything to me, Coy. I know how it is."

"You do?" he asked.

She nodded. "You enjoy attention from a lot of different girls. I get that. But that's not how I am. No, please let me finish; this isn't easy. We're too different. You like being the center of female adulation. I want a one woman type of guy, and I won't settle for anything less. I'm sure if there was ever anything between us, it was due to the extreme circumstances we found ourselves in for a few days, and will soon be forgotten. I came here for Cam, and I'm more certain than ever he's the right one for me."

She stood waiting for him to respond. She had to wait a long time until he at last found his voice.

"You're telling me you want Cam," he reiterated, to make sure he had it right.

She nodded.

"And anything we felt for each other is meaningless," he added.

She nodded again.

He stood and brushed the dust off his backside. Though she was tall, he now towered over her, and he looked very, very angry. "I was right about you from the beginning. You're a stone-cold ice princess. I'm sure you and my brother will do very well together. You both have ice water in your veins."

Ivy watched as he turned and stormed from the barn. A few minutes later his truck roared to life and then he rolled down the lane, leaving a cloud of dust in his wake.

CHAPTER 20

*I*vy couldn't sleep. Again. This time it wasn't because the space beside her felt empty, but rather because the space inside her felt empty. She had done it; she had finally decided between Coy and Cam. Why wasn't she happy? Was it because she had hurt Coy?

The look on his face as he turned away from her kept replaying in her head, over and over. If she was one in a long line of women, then why had he looked so devastated? Was that part of his act, too? Did he try to make each girl feel like she was special and the only girl for him? If so, he had the routine down pat. She couldn't get over the nagging sensation she had broken his heart, possibly irrevocably. But that was impossible, wasn't it? Guys like Coy, handsome guys who had a lot of experience, they didn't fall for backwards ball players who had barely ever dated before.

At some point she must have fallen asleep because the next thing she heard was a tap on her door.

"Ivy, it's Layla."

A quick glance of her clock showed it to be almost eight-thirty, an almost unheard of time to rise on a ranch. She stifled a groan and put her pillow over her head before realizing she needed to answer Layla.

130

"Yes," she said, hating the way her voice sounded heavy with telltale sleepiness.

"Cam wanted me to check on you. He said you were supposed to ride this morning but he had a few things to take care of. He'll return for you in an hour if that's okay."

"Okay. Thank you." After Layla shuffled away, Ivy jumped out of bed and into the shower. She took her time dressing and putting on her makeup, hoping if she looked perfect maybe it would make up for some of her embarrassing lapses in behavior lately.

"I'm never leaving Kentucky again," she muttered to her reflection. "No matter what my brothers do to me. I'll stay and take it until my hair turns gray and I die a lonely old woman." Belatedly she realized she was talking as if she and Cam weren't together when, in actuality, they were. She had officially chosen him, after all. There was the distinct possibility they could work out, get married, and Montana would be her new home. Coy would be her brother.

The mascara wand froze in midair, halfway to her eye as she thought that over. Well, she would cross that bridge when she got there. First things first, she had to leave this room and see Layla who no doubt thought she was a horrible person. First she had caught her canoodling with Coy on the couch, and now she had to wake her up practically in the middle of the day to go on a date with Cam.

Layla's hands were stuffed into a mound of dough when Ivy entered the kitchen. Layla was one of those industrious women who was always busy doing something. No doubt she had never slept so late in her entire life; one more reason for Ivy to feel sheepish. But some of her anxiety eased when Layla turned to give her a friendly smile.

"I'm sorry I slept so late," Ivy blurted.

Layla waved a hand, plopping a gob of dough on the counter. "Don't think a thing of it. I know you haven't been sleeping well since you got here." She bit her lip and turned toward the counter, obviously feeling awkward that she had brought up Ivy's sleeping arrangement from the night before.

"I'm sorry about that, too," Ivy said. "I don't know what's wrong with me. I haven't been myself since I arrived here."

"You can't sleep, don't want to eat, are confused, and can't concentrate," Layla said.

"Yes, how did you know?" Ivy sank into a chair.

"Sounds a lot like love," Layla replied, keeping her back to the table. "When Cade and I were getting together and trying to work out the kinks in our relationship, I was a mess. It was horrible and wonderful at the same time. He made me crazy."

"Things with Cam are good. He doesn't make me crazy," Ivy said placidly.

"I know," Layla said, shooting Ivy a look from the corner of her eye. "I wasn't talking about Cam."

Ivy bit her lip. "But I'm not, I mean that's, I've only known him for…And then there are all the other girls, and I…" She broke off with a helpless look.

"I don't know if this is helpful, but I can clear up a misconception for you. Girls love Coy. He has a boyish charm and innocent sweetness that hooks them like fish. But he doesn't do anything to seek their attention. It's not his fault they throw themselves at him. Yes, he's dated a lot, but he's never been serious about anyone. And not because he doesn't want to be. Even though he dates a lot, there's a part of himself he holds back, only allowing what's on the surface to show. True, he likes to have fun. But he's not a playboy or a user; he's been searching for the right girl."

"I told him I was choosing Cam," Ivy said slowly.

"Oh," Layla said. By her neutral tone Ivy couldn't tell what she was thinking. "I…Cam is the one I came here for. He and I have a rapport together we've worked hard to establish over the last year. We're friends, and we have similar business interests. He's…"

"Safe," Layla filled in for her. "Don't get me wrong—I love Cam. He's the big brother I never had. I think he's wonderful."

"But not for me," Ivy guessed.

"I didn't say that. It's really not my place to decide. You know yourself better than I know you. Both men are like brothers to me, and I love them. You really can't go wrong with either of them."

"But they could go horribly wrong with me," Ivy said despondently. On the basketball court, she had dominated, fearlessly taking on any opponents. But in the game of love, she was a hapless, insecure failure.

"I don't believe that," Layla said. "Besides the fact that you're beautiful, there's the practical aspect of your business. You're already acclimated to ranch life. You would do great here. On paper, you're a perfect match. I guess the real trick is figuring out what your heart wants."

"Thanks, Layla. This has been really nice. I'm not used to having a girl to talk to."

Layla smiled. "You're the first girl I've seen in two weeks."

Ivy returned her smile. "I guess we're sort of in the same boat, huh? One girl among so many men. There are a lot of women who would give anything to be in our shoes, but they have no idea how lonely it can be without anyone to talk girl talk with."

"You can talk girl talk with me anytime," Layla said. "I'm starved for it. Last week Cade went to the store and I asked him to pick me up some mascara. He came back with black shoe polish. No lie. He thought it was the bulk version and he was saving some money. I'm *starving* for some female commiseration."

Ivy put her arm over her stomach and laughed. "If I ever come back, we'll spend a whole day doing our hair and makeup. That's my favorite thing about being a girl."

Layla dropped her dough, a dreamy expression on her face. "Talking to someone who knows the difference between blush and bronzer sounds like a dream come true."

"Doesn't it, though?" Cam asked from the doorway. He turned to Ivy. "I finished a little early. Are you ready?"

"She hasn't eaten yet," Layla answered for her.

"I'll take a cookie to go, if you don't mind," Layla said. Eating straight sugar for breakfast was a bad idea, but she didn't want to keep

Cam waiting any longer. Her stomach was already filled with butterflies over the upcoming ride. Her decision to choose him over Coy made her feel more connected to him. Would he sense that connection? Would he finally make a move and test the chemistry between them?

The butterflies kicked into high gear. What if he kissed her and it was bad? Would she always wonder how a kiss with Coy might have been different? But then what if he kissed her and it was good? Would it erase any thoughts or traces of Coy?

One thing was for certain, it could prove to be an interesting ride.

* * *

COY WAS EXHAUSTED. For the first time in a long time, he hadn't slept at home. Instead, he had driven three hours the night before on the pretense of visiting his old friend, Dobbie. Of course not until he reached his ranch on the south side of the neighboring county did he realize he had forgotten to call and wrangle an invitation. Still, Dobbie seemed unfazed by his arrival, but he was laid back that way.

His wife, Libby, also made him feel welcome.

"Come in and eat," she said, opening the screen door wide and beckoning him with her arm outstretched. "I can't get used to cooking for just us since my sisters moved away. I always prepare too much."

Indeed, when he saw the table he realized she hadn't been exaggerating. The table fairly groaned under the delicious-looking meal. If he didn't know better, he might think she had foreknowledge of his visit because everything was laid out in fine china. Formal napkins lay on the table in some sort of intricate-looking fold. All in all, it looked like a meal prepared for a magazine shoot. Coy felt slightly intimidated by the sight, but not by Libby's warm and welcoming manner.

Then he noted she was wearing a dress, and he paused. "Are you sure I'm not interrupting something?" he asked.

"This is how we eat every night," Dobbie said, grinning. "Tell me again how whipped I am."

Deciding to ignore him, Coy turned his attention to Libby. "Where did your sisters go?"

"My oldest sister lives in Pittsburgh. She passed the bar last month. My other two sisters live in Omaha and Brooklyn, respectively."

"Brooklyn?" he quirked an eyebrow. "I have a friend from high school who lives in Manhattan." For an instant, he wondered if they might know each other, then he realized he was thinking like a Montana native. Though the state was vast, there were few people. Their world was small, and it was always easy to find someone who knew someone you knew, especially among the ranching families. New York was Montana's opposite; the space was small, but the population was dense. It was most likely possible to live there all one's life and never meet the neighbors.

After supper he spent a few minutes playing with Libby and Dobbie's baby, Celia. Coy secretly thought unless something changed, Libby would be the disciplinarian in their family because Celia had Dobbie wrapped around her little finger. She also had her mother's eye for aesthetics because she carefully lined up all her blocks so they were all facing the same direction, and then cried if any of them fell over, ruining her tower.

Though they had no foreknowledge of his abrupt arrival, Libby and Dobbie invited him to stay the night. After apologizing profusely for dropping in so unexpectedly, he gave in and stayed. The sheets looked too pretty to touch, let alone to sleep on, but he slept anyway for the first time in a couple of weeks. The next morning, he inspected a few acres of the ranch with Dobbie, complimenting him on some improvements he had made. Though the ranch was a tenth the size of the King's ranch, it was well run and efficient, making it profitable even when prices fell, as they were apt to do lately.

They spent a while talking politics, and then it was time for Coy to leave.

"Thanks for taking me in like this, Dobbie. I know I must seem like a crazy person dropping in on you. Give my thanks to Libby."

"Libby is always glad to have visitors; we both are. You're welcome anytime, King. Maybe next time you can bring this girl who's giving you so much trouble. Libby would enjoy the company."

Coy's gut twisted as he thought about how much he would enjoy having Ivy spend time with his friends. Instinctively he knew she and Libby would hit it off. "I don't see that happening any time soon. She gave me the boot."

Dobbie smiled. "Did she? I wouldn't be too sure. I have a feeling about these things."

Coy laughed. "You're a dusty old cowboy and you have a *feeling* about love?"

"I also grew up here with four girls. They have a way of rubbing off on you and making you think like them sometimes." He shuddered. "I'm starting to sound like my brother-in-law. He's practically a girl himself."

"Well, I think your feeling is wrong on this one, but thank you all the same. And if you, Libby, and Celia ever want to see what you're missing up north, come and visit us anytime."

"We might do that. Libby's been hinting she wants to get away before the new baby arrives, and I've never seen your spread."

"It's official then." He tugged his Stetson, hopped in his truck, and began the journey home. Though their two counties touched each other, the Chapman ranch was at the south end of their county, and the King ranch was on the north side of their county, making the drive much longer than it should have been.

In order to stop his mind from rehashing all he didn't want to think about, he found an AM talk radio station and tried to focus on it. But his traitorous brain wouldn't cooperate.

How could Ivy have dropped him like that? And how could he stand by and watch her with Cam?

The answer to that was simple; he couldn't. Seeing Dobbie reminded him Dobbie had also faced a personal crisis and gone away for a couple of years. Coy could do the same. Ranches always needed workers. It might be nice to see some other places in the country. He had heard good things about Wyoming. Maybe he would head there.

And, while he was on the subject, why wait? He didn't have to linger on the ranch, waiting for Cam and Ivy to get serious, dying a little more each day until their inevitable wedding. He could pack up and leave anytime he wanted.

He gripped the steering wheel tighter. The thought of leaving was at once terrifying and freeing. He could go, but at what price? Since Cade's accident, the remaining brothers had added more physical labor to pick up the slack. His leaving would make things even worse.

But with the potential income from Ivy's horse business, they could afford to hire as many people as they wanted, he thought bitterly. He could picture the little business empire Cam and Ivy would build together. No doubt they would be all business all the time.

Yes, he would go away. Tonight, if possible. He would get on the train, pick a random destination, and find a job.

With that thought in mind, he stomped to the office in order to tell Cam his plan. It was a no-brainer he would find Cam in the office; he rarely left it, and this afternoon was no exception.

"I need to talk to you," Coy announced, throwing down his hat like the proverbial gauntlet.

"Not yet," Cam said, not looking up from his ledger.

"Yes, now," Coy said, angrier than he had ever been. He had no idea why he should be angry at Cam except that the woman he loved loved him, and that was maddening.

"I was hoping you would check on Ivy first," Cam said, grabbing Coy's attention so he froze and stared at the top of his twin's head.

"What?" he asked dumbly. "Why would Ivy need checked on?"

Cam put down his pen and looked up. "Because I broke up with her."

CHAPTER 21

"You what?" Coy staggered back into the chair, remembering to grab his hat a split second before he crushed it.

"I broke up with Ivy."

"Why?" Coy asked. Why would anyone in his right mind break up with Ivy?

Cam shrugged. "I'm not in love with her. On paper, the formula works. But it turns out you were right; you need chemistry. We had no chemistry."

Coy blinked rapidly, trying to process the words. "Why are you telling me to check on her?"

"Because you're in love with her," Cam said. "And I'm pretty sure she's in love with you."

Coy's only answer was to blink some more. "You know?" he asked at last.

"This is my ranch; I know everything," Cam said. Though they had always been equally matched in size and strength, Coy had never been able to suppress a shudder of fear when Cam spoke that way—as if he had super powers and could read minds. Sometimes Coy wondered if he actually could.

He sank into his chair. "I didn't mean to fall in love with her."

"I know. Being trapped together for so long will have that effect, I guess."

"No, I mean, maybe, but I think maybe I would have fallen for her anyway. She's the right girl for me, I think. The only girl." He broke off, realizing how he must sound to Cam. "So what happens now?"

"I guess that's up to you. Do you want her or not?"

"Oh, I want her."

"Then go get her," Cam said. He dropped his eyes to the ledger again, effectively dismissing Coy.

"But I don't think she wants me. She already told me so."

"Then change her mind," Cam said, not looking up from his book.

Coy wanted to ask how, but he couldn't. He had already crossed lines brothers should never cross. Asking his brother how to woo his ex-girlfriend was even farther than he was willing to go. He stood.

"Are we okay?"

"We will be," Cam said. He kept his head down while Coy exited the room, then he threw down his pen and scowled at the door. The thought of running away had never been more appealing. He wasn't hurt Coy and Ivy had fallen in love; he wasn't even angry. But he was humiliated.

Everyone in town knew he had brought Ivy here. Now everyone in town would know she preferred Coy to him. The sting of her rejection was about to be public knowledge, and Cam was unprepared to deal with the ensuing laughter and humiliation. From this point forward, he would always be known as the brother who came in second place—a status he had been fighting all his life.

From his earliest memories, people had preferred Coy to him. He had never had the easy smiles and pleasant manners of his twin. Even as a baby, he had been serious and ill tempered. Some of his earliest memories were the trips his family took to town. Without fail, people stopped and gushed over Coy with barely a glance at him.

He wasn't so shallow or needy that it bothered him a lot. But it did bother him a little, and that little bit annoyed him. For once, and when it was most important, he wanted to be the chosen brother. He wanted a woman to fall in love with him because she wanted him, and not because Coy was already taken.

After one more sigh, he picked up his pen. He wouldn't run away. He wouldn't pout. He wouldn't even allow himself another thought on the subject. What was done was done, and there was work to be done —like always.

* * *

Coy saw her sitting in the rocking chair on the front porch. Even from this far away, he could tell she was upset. He froze mid-stride. Was she crying because she was so upset over Cam's loss? Or were her tears simply from the rejection and confusion she had endured since her arrival here? After the turmoil of the last two weeks, he wouldn't blame her if she ran away and never set foot on the ranch again.

Panic seized his heart. What if she did? What if she went away and never came back? She had already rejected him once, what if she rejected him again?

Movement caught Ivy's eye. Listlessly, she turned her head to the side and saw Coy exit the office like a madman. She wondered where he could possibly be headed in such a hurry and then it hit her; he was headed for her.

His hat was in his hands as he strode toward her. He had apparently put it on while his hair was still damp because there was a ring of flattened hair on the top of his head. All around the ends curled up, and she had the sudden desire to put her fingers in his hair and fluff the curls back to life.

He reached her, and she stood. Before she could stop herself, she did what she had been thinking about; she reached up and fluffed his hair, making the flattened pieces spring to life with fresh curls. She smiled at the curls, realizing how much she enjoyed them.

Coy watched her warily. Why was she smiling at his hair? Although, at this point any sort of smile was a good sign.

"Ivy," he started. He tossed his hat onto the chair and gripped her biceps, drawing her closer. But before he could continue, they were alerted by the sound of a car traveling up the driveway. The lane was dirt and gravel, so cars usually took it at a snail's pace. Not this car, though. It flew. And it wasn't a car, but a large, black SUV, honking like crazy.

Ivy glanced at the car and stifled a scream, slapping her hand to her mouth in horror. "They're here," she rasped.

Coy didn't have to ask who "they" were. The brothers had come at last. The vehicle screeched to a halt in front of the house as if they were in the middle of filming a *Fast and Furious* movie. He had always thought himself to be courageous, but when the doors sprang open, all four at once, and five brothers spilled out like some super-sized version of a clown car on steroids, he had the sudden desire to turn and bolt.

At six feet, Coy considered himself tall. But the shortest brother was at least five inches taller than him. They all had black eyes and they were all covered in black hair, seemingly from head to toe. On their heads, the hair was cropped close, but there was no taming the hair on their arms, legs, and even their chests. Tufts of hair popped over their shirts, mesmerizing Coy. Neither he nor any of his brothers had chest hair. Did they have hair on their backs, too? He fervently hoped never to find out. *Please don't ever let me see one of them without a shirt on,* he silently prayed.

He supposed girls would probably find them attractive, despite the hair. They looked like a band of dangerous pirates, although they were all clean and appeared to have their own teeth, limbs, and eyes. But Coy didn't find them attractive; he found them terrifying. No wonder Ivy had never dated much. A man would have to be insanely in love with her to go up against this bunch. The fact that he was insanely in love with her gave him the courage he needed to hold his ground and face them.

"Are you the Yankee who stole our baby sister?" the tallest one demanded, his voice booming through the ranch like a canon. The five brothers made a line in front of Coy. One of them pounded his fist into his palm, and another cracked his knuckles, stretching his neck back and forth.

Ivy opened her mouth to speak. Coy let go of her biceps and draped his arm on her shoulder. "Sweetheart, don't get upset. You know what the doctor said." Turning to the brothers, he forced a smile. "This is my fault. Don't blame Ivy. I knew as soon as you heard about the wedding you would show up here. She wanted to wait until her family could be here for the ceremony, but I was anxious to get it over with. And you have to admit the circumstances caused us to rush. I want our baby to have my name when he gets here." He pressed his palm possessively to Ivy's stomach.

Across from him, the brothers stood dumbstruck, all five of their oversized jaws dropping at once. The tallest one might actually have growled. Five pairs of eyes darted frantically between Ivy and Coy. Ivy played her part well, pressing her hand over Coy's and giving him an adoring look, one that took zero acting on her part.

Turning back to her brothers, she spoke. "I told Mom not to tell you about the wedding and the baby. I wanted to tell you myself, in person. Surprise!"

They remained speechless, though their muscles all seemed to be bunching at the same time, as if ready to spring into action as one joined unit.

"Why don't we all go inside?" Coy suggested, his sunny tone a stark contrast to their mutinous features. "I think our housekeeper baked some cookies. You guys must be hungry."

The tallest one finally found his voice, a deep baritone that would have sparked terror into a lesser man. "That sounds real nice, Yankee, but it's going to have to wait until we take turns killing you." He took a step forward.

Fleetingly, Coy wondered who would come out on top in a fight between the Kings and the Honeywells. True, the Honeywells were huge, and there were five of them. But the Kings could hold their own, and no doubt Layla and Ivy would join in the fray. He was almost looking forward to the opportunity to find out what would happen when Ivy moved away from him and spoke, hands perched on hips so her anger temporarily matched that of her brothers.

"Oh stop it, you goons. I've been here for two weeks. How on earth could I get pregnant and married in that time? He was teasing you. And this isn't even Cam. This is his brother Coy. We're not together. I'm not with anyone," she said. Her voice choked on the last word. She fled from the porch steps, pushing through the line of her brothers, and then she ran to the barn.

Coy watched her go with a frown, desperate to tag after her and make things right. He took a step toward the barn when one of the brothers placed a meaty paw on his shoulder, anchoring him in place.

"Please tell me you were being serious about the cookies," another of the brothers demanded.

Coy nodded vaguely, his eyes still trained on Ivy's retreating form. "Help yourselves," he said, gesturing toward the house. They filed past him in silence.

"Good one," the tallest one said, pausing to look down on Coy with a calculated smile. "But, seriously, touch our sister again and we will kill you." The door slammed behind them. Coy descended the steps, belatedly realizing he should have warned Layla about the five gorillas who had entered her house. He wondered what they said to her because she screamed loudly and dropped what sounded like a frying pan on the floor.

The door of the office flew open and Cade began wheeling himself furiously down the ramp.

"Was that Layla? What happened? What's wrong?" he asked.

"Ivy's brothers are here," Coy said. Cade paused and regarded the house. "You'd better keep going. I don't trust them alone with her." He wouldn't put it past them to kidnap her and take her back to Kentucky for kicks, especially because she was pretty.

"Are they as bad as Ivy made them sound?" Cade asked.

"They're worse," Coy answered before continuing his journey to the horse barn.

Ivy was nowhere in sight. Coy stopped in the entryway and scanned the barn, but he couldn't find her.

"Ivy," he called softly. There was no answer. Had she slipped out the back of the barn when he stopped to talk to Cade? He turned to go, and then he heard it, a soft snuffling sound coming from one of the stalls. He followed the sound until he located her crouched in the far horse stall, a kitten clutched tightly to her face.

He said her name softly and she jumped, startling the kitten so it yowled plaintively. His heart lurched when her tearstained face tipped up to peer at him through the kitten's fur. For a few beats, they looked at each other. He held out his hand to her. Slowly, she set the kitten aside and stood, her eyes never leaving his. She took one tentative step toward him, and suddenly the barn was filled with sounds that echoed off the walls causing the horses to shimmy nervously in their stalls.

"They found us," Ivy whispered, her voice choked with dread.

Coy had no reply, but the sinking feeling in his chest told him whatever happened next wasn't going to be good. His fear was confirmed when a hand clamped heavily on his shoulder and squeezed.

"You're coming with us, Yankee."

A different hand clamped on his other shoulder, and together they began dragging him backwards.

"Later," he mouthed to Ivy.

She blinked at him. Her eyes round with worry and fear, as if she thought she might be seeing him for the last time.

"Where are you taking me?" he asked when the brothers roughly manhandled him into their rented SUV.

"Your brother told us about the OLWS breeder. We thought we would have a little word with him. You're going to show us where he lives."

"He lives two hours away," Coy answered. If he thought that news would dissuade them from their purpose, he was sadly mistaken. In a panic now, he looked for an escape, but there was none. Large and formidable brothers blocked the exit on each side of him. Instead of trying to make a break for it, he turned to look out the back window, hoping for a glimpse of Ivy.

She stood at the edge of the barn. One hand clutching a kitten tightly to her chest, while her other hand remained outstretched in a suspended, beseeching wave. Coy pressed his hand against the back door as he realized he was captive.

CHAPTER 22

The feeling he was being held prisoner didn't dissipate as the miles flew. The brothers remained silent and stoic, facing forward with their hands folded in their laps as if their positions had been prearranged before their departure. Coy expected them to ask him directions to the breeder's house, but they didn't. Either Cade gave them directions, or they innately knew where bad horses were being reared because they drove straight to the breeder's ranch without making one wrong turn.

"Let us do the talking," the tallest one said as he hauled Coy from the vehicle by his shirt collar.

Coy shook him off and fought the urge to punch him. He wasn't accustomed to being manhandled or told what to do. But since he was attempting to make a good impression, he held his tongue.

He followed Ivy's brothers like an errant puppy; much shorter and smaller, he remained well-hidden behind the behemoth brothers. The tallest brother rapped sharply on the door of the house. They stood shuffling impatiently, waiting for an answer. When none came, they turned and stormed to the barn, Coy trailing in their wake.

There was no one in the barn either, but that didn't stop the brothers from barging into the stable as they spread out and began checking the horses. Coy watched, undeniably fascinated, as they ran expert hands over flanks, looking for telltale signs of poor breeding. By their combined huffs and harrumphs, he was sure they found many.

"Who the devil are you, and what the devil are you doing?" Arthur Henry, the breeder in question, entered the barn predictably outraged.

"The devil indeed," one of the brothers said, his low voice skittering around the barn like a warning. At some point Coy must really learn their names. They came together to form a line as they descended on Arthur.

He backed up a step and searched frantically, probably for his gun. Absently, Coy wondered if bullets had any effect on the brothers. Maybe, like the grizzly bears they resembled, they would require a high-powered rifle and special ammunition in order to dent their hides.

"Who are you people?" Arthur asked, his voice a croaky whisper.

One of the brothers produced a wallet and flipped it open. "Livery and game commission. We came to investigate a faulty foal you sold to the King ranch." He flipped his wallet closed and stuffed it in his pocket.

Arthur's wild eyes fastened on Coy. "I had no idea that foal had OLWS," he insisted.

"Exactly," one of the brothers said. As a unit they took another step closer to Arthur who cowered, now clutching the wall behind him for support. "A simple genetic test would have prevented such waste."

"Those tests are expensive," Arthur defended, nervously licking his lips.

"Not as expensive as the loss of your business," one of the brothers said.

"You wouldn't…you couldn't," Arthur sputtered. He threw another helpless look at Coy who shrugged in return. He had to admit he was enjoying Arthur's dismay. After what Cam had unearthed about his shoddy breeding practices, Arthur was due for some comeuppance.

"We would. We could," the largest brother said. "Here's what's going to happen: you're going to test each and every one of your horses, and if two are carriers for the OLWS gene, you won't breed them together. Got it?"

Arthur nodded dazedly.

"If you don't comply, we'll know. As soon as we're sure you've done the proper testing, we're going to come back and talk some more about proper breeding practices."

"You have no legal right to…" Arthur tried again, but a brother cut him off.

"We have a moral responsibility to see that your horses are well taken care of. We know people who know people and, believe me, you don't want to see what happens if you don't do as you're told."

Without waiting to see what reaction their words had, the brothers filed past him and bustled into the SUV.

"Here, boy," one of them called, beckoning for Coy with a slap to his thigh, as if calling an errant puppy.

Coy and Arthur exchanged mutually helpless looks as they passed each other.

"Who are they?" Arthur hissed, voice thick with panic.

"My future in-laws," Coy said, tone dismal, and then he was roughly jerked back into the SUV as it headed down the long dusty lane.

Despite the ordeal, his sense of relief was palpable. In two hours he would be back at his ranch, back with Ivy, and away from her psychotic brothers.

However, the brothers had other plans, and Coy's relief was short-lived.

"Where are you going?" he asked when they turned in the opposite direction of the ranch.

"To get wheelchairs," one of the brothers answered, not sparing him a glance.

Coy paused a few beats, trying to decide if he had heard correctly. "Wheelchairs?" he repeated at last. "Why wheelchairs?"

"Cade said he plays basketball in his chair. We want to see what that's like."

Coy blinked at them. "But Cade gets his chairs from Billings. That's another three hours away."

"So it is." This came from the brother who was driving.

"We can't go to Billings," Coy said.

"Sure we can," a brother answered.

And that was that. Three hours later, they pulled into the medical supply store in Billings. An hour of heated negotiations later, the brothers bought five wheelchairs and loaded them into the already crowded SUV.

Coy was beyond caring, even though he had to sit with his body contorted around two chairs that poked and prodded him uncomfortably. The brothers seemed to regard him the same as they regarded the chairs, packing all of them together haphazardly in the back of the SUV. Coy didn't mind; compressed as he was, it was still better than sharing space with the goon squad up front. All he cared about was getting back to the ranch and Ivy, to make things right between them. He relaxed as much as he could until he noticed the direction the SUV was heading.

"Where are we going now?" If his voice sounded like a plaintive whine, he thought he was well within his rights.

"Supper," a brother announced. "And then we'll find a hotel."

"No." Coy struggled to sit up, pushing aside chairs as he did so, buried beneath them as he was. It hadn't passed his notice that they tossed him in first, absently piling the five chairs on top of him as if they were the more precious cargo. "Absolutely not. Turn the car around."

Of course they ignored him.

He fought his way through the maze of chairs and launched himself over the two seats that separated him from the front of the car. The brothers made no move to get out of his way, but he didn't care. He stepped on them, sure nothing could wound them. When he was at last within reach of the steering wheel, he grabbed hold and tugged.

The brother who was driving didn't release his grip, nor did he ease up his foot on the gas pedal. Instead the vehicle careened wildly from side to side as he and Coy played tug of war with the steering wheel. Fleetingly Coy wondered if he would survive another plunge over a ravine. Undoubtedly the brothers would walk away unscathed like the robots in *Terminator*.

"We're going back to the ranch," Coy announced.

"Why?" a brother asked. He made no move to dislodge Coy from the steering wheel or help his brother try to control the vehicle. Instead he leaned forward interestedly, as if he couldn't wait to see the outcome of their struggle.

"Because I need to talk to Ivy," Coy said, jerking the wheel once again.

"What do you need to talk to Ivy about?" another brother asked as the car veered wildly to the left, narrowly avoiding the gravel at the side of the road.

"None of your business," Coy said. His teeth were tightly gritted, both in anger and exertion as he tried to keep himself upright while stretched the length of the vehicle.

"Guess again," a brother said. "Everything that concerns our baby sister is our business."

"She's not a baby." Sweat beads formed on Coy's brow, but he had no free hands to wipe them away. "And she's tired of you interfering in her life." He grunted as he spotted a road up ahead. Tugging with all his might, he tried to make the car turn, but the brother in charge of the wheel wouldn't relent. How was it possible for a man to be so freakishly strong? Coy was a rancher, for goodness sake. What could the brothers possibly do that was harder than that?

"Well that's not going to stop," a brother said. "Ever."

"Someday she'll be married," Coy said.

"So? We're part of the package."

"I'm learning that the hard way," Coy said.

The SUV came to an abrupt halt. Coy didn't. He careened forward until his head connected with the dashboard, striking the goose egg that was still tender from his last encounter with a car part.

Coy landed on the floor with a heavy thud before rolling over to look up. Five Cro-Magnon brows peered down at him, assessing him in ominous silence.

"You want Ivy?" one asked at last.

"Yes," Coy said, wincing as he tried not to gasp. It wasn't merely that the dashboard had knocked the wind from him, but he was also now folded in half like a pretzel on the bottom of the SUV.

"Ivy doesn't come free." He had no idea which one said that; they were all starting to homogenize and blend together. Maybe there was only one of them and he was really good at moving quickly so it appeared as if there were others. Coy had lost the ability to tell anymore. Reality and fantasy were beginning to blend and he began to fear they might actually have some sort of supernatural powers. Had there been some sort of pact with the devil that made them so large and indestructible?

He frowned. "You want me to pay you?"

"Not with money," a brother answered, the first hint of amusement entering his tone.

Coy shuddered, not liking the wicked gleam in the brothers' eyes.

CHAPTER 23

The next morning Coy found Ivy sitting on the rail of the last stall. She was watching the mare that had delivered the OLWS foal.

"I think she's sad," Ivy said when he approached.

He thought *she* was sad. Her cheeks were wet with telltale traces of tears, and there were raccoon-like smudges under each eye. Plus she sniffled a couple of times.

"And I am never going on vacation again," she added emphatically when he failed to make a response.

"Has it really been so bad?" he asked gently, resting his arms against the gate.

"Let me try and choose my favorite part: was it being stranded in the wilderness for three days with no food or water? Or maybe it was being dumped by the guy I came to visit. Or, hmm, maybe it was the unexpected arrival of the Honeywell thug squad. I apparently can't get away from them no matter where I go." Another tear slowly leaked out and she swiped it away.

"Yes, but you met me," Coy added lightly.

Her lower lip jutted like she might cry again. "Please don't joke, Coy."

"I'm not joking, Ivy." He moved closer, put his arm around her waist, and pulled her back slightly so she rested against his chest, putting his lips softly against her ear. "Tell me there's nothing between us."

"Of course there is," she said, her tender tone unconsciously matching his. She couldn't resist the impulse to reach her hand up and touch his curls again, sifting her fingers through them. "But there seems to be something between you and every other girl on the planet."

"That's not true," he said gently. "There have been a lot of girls, but no one special. No one like you."

She closed her eyes and tipped her head so it rested against his. She so badly wanted to believe him, but she was afraid. What if she took a step of faith, and she was wrong? What if he dumped her for someone else and broke her heart?

"How do I know?" she asked. "How can I be sure I can trust you?"

"Why else would I have been willing to let your brothers make mincemeat of me if I didn't love you?" She opened her mouth to speak again, but he didn't give her the chance. Putting his hand on the back of her head, he drew her closer and kissed her.

The kiss, slow and gentle though it was, had the desired effect of erasing any traces of doubt from her mind. She loved this man. For better or worse, even if he broke her heart, she wanted to be with him.

"Plus there's that," Coy said shakily when the kiss finished. "I've never had that kind of chemistry with anyone else. And you're still the prettiest thing I've ever seen. Don't walk away, Ivy. Don't be scared." He traced her cheek with his fingers. "Take a chance on me, on Montana, on *us*."

She opened her eyes, a smile slowly spreading. "How could I say no to the only man who has ever stumped my brothers? Did you see the looks on their faces when you told them I was pregnant? For as long as I live, I will never forget that moment, the moment you made them speechless for once in my life." She squeezed his hand, beaming.

He smiled in return. "You know what would really kill them? If you actually married me. Today. Montana doesn't have a waiting period. Think how they would react if we slipped away to the courthouse and came back married."

Her eyes rounded with excitement as she imagined pulling something so big over on her overbearing, know-it-all brothers. Then her shoulders slumped with defeat. "We can't get married to trick my brothers," she said.

"Then how about we get married because I want to be with you every day for the rest of our lives? How about because I love you? How about because I don't want to spend one more minute with an empty bed. I had no idea how much I hated sleeping alone until I met you. The space feels empty without you." His hand brushed over her silky feel, causing electric sparks to jump between them from the contact.

She sat up excitedly again, clutching his shirt in both her hands. Could she actually do this? Could she go to the courthouse right now and get married? Surprisingly she found she wanted to, except for one small thing: "My parents. I want my parents to be at our wedding. I want my dad to give me away, and I want to be married at my home church in Kentucky."

"That's not a no," he drawled.

"It's not a no," she agreed. "It's a yes. No, wait. It's a yes, please and thank you."

He gathered her closer, and now he was the one who was beaming as he leaned closer to whisper. He had no proof the brothers could hear everything, but it seemed so. "You know, we could slip away and fly to Kentucky right now. I can call Cade and tell him to keep your brothers busy while we make our getaway."

"I love that idea," she agreed enthusiastically, squirming with excitement. Her cheeks flushed the loveliest shade of pink, and it was all he could do not to stop and stare at the pretty picture she made. *Mine,* his heart thought, thudding hard. *Mine forever.*

He led her to the office, picked up the phone, and called the house. Cade answered on the third ring.

"How's it going with the brothers?" Coy asked.

"They're in Ivy's room now. I don't know what they're doing, but they're hammering something. I don't say this often, but I'm afraid. Please make them go away from here."

"Do me a favor and keep them busy for a while. Ivy and I are flying to Kentucky."

There was a pause for a few beats. "What about her things?"

"Ship them after the brothers leave. Whatever you do, do not let them follow us."

"I guess I could play wheelchair basketball with them. Do you think they'll foul a guy in a wheelchair?"

Coy thought of the horrific night he had spent with the brothers and shuddered. It would be a long time before he could speak of the things that had passed between them. "They won't kill you," he said unconvincingly. "Probably."

"Are you ever going to tell me why they kept you out all night or why you were limping and rope burned when you finally stumbled home this morning?" Cade asked.

"You wouldn't believe me if I told you," Coy said. Memories of the physical and emotional endurance tests the brothers had made him suffer were still too fresh in his mind to rehash. Maybe some day he would be able to talk about what had passed in the night, but not right now. Not right now. He shuddered again, causing Ivy to smooth her hand up and down his arm in worried concern.

"There's one more thing," Coy added, returning his attention to Cade. "Decide among yourselves who's going to be my best man. We're getting married in two weeks." He glanced at Ivy to make sure the date was all right with her and smiled when she was unfazed. "Oh, and Cade, when our absence is discovered, give the brothers a message for me: tell them 'Welcome to Montana.'" He smiled as he hung up the phone, then he swept Ivy off her feet and carried her to his truck.

A little over one year later, Coy and Ivy's house was finally finished. They had lived in the main house with the other brothers and Layla until the original homestead could be remodeled for them. Although the main house was large and they loved their family, they were ready for a space of their own.

"I love it," Ivy said as they stood on the lawn, staring at their new house. It was a ranch house, much smaller than the main house, but plenty large enough for them and their future children. The outside was wooden clapboard, and Ivy had lovingly chosen the perfect shade of ivory. In addition to starting her new horse-breeding business with the mare and stallion her father gave her as a wedding present, she had kept busy overseeing every detail of the renovation. She had no idea she was such a demanding taskmistress until the project involved her dream home. Then no detail was too small for her to worry about.

"Let's make it official," Coy said. Sweeping an arm under her knees, he picked her up and carried her over the threshold. Once safely inside, he shut the door with his foot, then reached back and locked it.

"Are you afraid of robbers since we moved a few hundred feet away from the others?" Ivy teased.

"No, I'm afraid of family interrupting us during our first night in our new house."

"Good thinking," Ivy said. "Slide the bolt."

In the morning, Coy woke early. He stared bleary-eyed at the coffee pot, mentally commanding it to brew faster. Once it was finally finished, he decided to take advantage of the gracious front porch Ivy had designed by having his coffee outside. He still felt half asleep as he stumbled outside, which was why it took him a few minutes of stunned silence to make sure he was actually seeing what he thought he was seeing.

The house that had only yesterday been a soft shade of ivory was now a deep midnight blue. He backed up off the porch so he could see the house in full. Were his eyes playing tricks on him? No, the house was actually blue now.

It was when he was ascending the porch steps again he saw the note taped to the door. He picked it up and read it to himself.

"Dear Yankee Rebel, Here's a little reminder from the bluegrass state of what happens when you steal our baby sister. PS. WE'RE WATCHING YOU."

Coy stood up straighter, head whipping back and forth. Did they mean that literally? Were they somewhere nearby watching his reaction? How had they known the house was finished? How had they known this was their first night in the new house? And, most importantly, *how had they completely repainted the house in the middle of the night without making a sound?*

He fought the urge to shudder. The thought he was being watched made him want to black out all the windows and keep a radio on at all times for white noise. Not that he had any intention of ever mistreating Ivy, but there were other, more intimate moments he didn't want his brothers-in-law to know about, much less witness.

"Morning, Sweetie," Ivy said. She sounded as groggy as he had felt a few minutes ago. She stood on her toes, leaning in to smell his coffee and steal a kiss, and then she paused, staring at him. "What's wrong?"

He hadn't yet worked out the tricky problem of how to break the news to her, so he simply pointed toward the house.

She whirled to look and let out a high-pitched scream of rage. "I'm going to kill them," she said. "Literally this time. I am going to hunt each one of them down and end his life. I'll use a rhino tranquilizer gun to take them down if I have to. How could they do this? I've never been so mad in my entire life." To prove her point, she burst into loud, angry tears.

"Ivy, honey, it's okay. We still have some paint from the remodel. My brothers and I can have this place repainted by the end of the day." If the Honeywell brothers could paint an entire house in a night, he and his brothers could surely repaint it in a day. Couldn't they?

"It's not that," she said between hiccupping sobs. She pressed her hand over her eyes, trying without success to push back the tears. "I've been expecting something like this for months now. I'm crying because I like this color better." She added her other hand over her face and cried harder.

"Oh," he said warily, unsure how to proceed. "Well, good. If you like this color better we can keep it."

"We can't keep it," she wailed. "They'll know we kept it because I like it, and they'll rub my face in it forever."

"We'll tell them *I* like the blue color better and want to keep it. They'll hate that."

She sniffed and looked up at him. "They will hate that. That's a great idea. I knew I loved you for good reason." She stood on her toes to kiss him, but before she could reach him Josh bolted out of the main house and ran full speed toward them.

"This can't be good," Coy muttered.

Josh came to a screeching halt as he took in the new blue color of the house. He shook his head as if to clear it and looked at Coy and Ivy. "Coy, the sheriff called. Your truck is on the top of the high school. And it's blue now." He stopped speaking and stared at the house again with a puzzled frown.

"I'm going to kill them," Coy said.

"I have a better idea," Ivy said. "They took the truck without your permission, right? So let's contact the sheriff and file a complaint for unauthorized use. A warrant for their arrest will keep them from coming back for a while."

Coy smiled. "You've been looking for a reason to swear out an arrest warrant for them, haven't you?"

"Pretty much since I was born. And I have you to thank for providing me with a reason." This time she did stand on her toes to kiss him.

Josh turned and walked back to the house thinking he would never understand women as long as he lived. At least Cam was still on his side. Maybe the love bug had gotten to Coy and Cade, but they had never been very sensible to begin with. He was certain that, no matter what the future held, nothing would happen to change him or Cam. Not a girl, not love, not anything.

With that happy thought in mind, he whistled as he went to the barn to check on his new puppy.

THANK you for reading *Cowboy Lost*, the second book in the Kings of Montana Series. For more on the Honeywell brothers, please check out the five book series, the Honeywells of Kentucky. And for more books, please check out my website www.vanessagraybartal.com